ENCORE

SAVING ABBIE BOOK 6

MAGGIE ALABASTER

JO BRADLEY

Cover by Book Brander

Edited by Lily Luchesi

Proofread by Nora Hogan

Bond
  Written by Channing Griffin

Slip the blade,
  Draw the line,
  Feel the blood,
  Take the end.
  The end.

Step too far,
  Slip too deep,
  Drip too hard,
  Scream too loud.
  Too loud.

Take my hand,
  Squeeze my throat,
  Hold my soul,
  Steal my light.
  My light.

Love that hard,
  Feel that much,
  Take that step,
  Tie that bond.

Tie that bond.
That bond.

ABBIE

BREATHE IN.

Breathe out.

I forced myself to suck in oxygen. Blood pounded through my ears. Loud as fuck. Not loud enough to drown out the thoughts that raced through my head. Not loud enough to block out the truth.

I wanted to scream until I couldn't hear them anymore. I wanted to dive under a scalding hot shower and wash them away. I wanted to go back a couple of minutes to a time before I heard what Channing and the evil twins said.

Nothing would erase it now.

Nothing.

Last night's dinner curdled in my stomach, threatening to come back up. I was living in the epicentre of a nightmare and I didn't understand any of it.

Channing was a killer.

Channing.

The saxophonist for Wolf Venom was far from innocent, I knew that, but this— this was something entirely different. Something I never in a million years would have expected to hear.

But at the same time, I knew it was true. It all made sense. What I didn't understand, couldn't get my head around, was why.

Why had Channing killed Jonah, Poppy Newton, Vance, Calista Rossi and possibly Pete? To protect us?

Fuck, did he really think—

"What the hell?" Landon whispered. He sounded gutted, shocked.

In the faint glow of a streetlight, I saw his face, pale beneath his tan, his eyes wide. He looked as horrified as I felt, as blindsided. When I thought he might deny what we heard, he didn't.

"I don't know, shhh," Jackson urged. He had an arm around each of us, his hands on our backs, keeping us down low. For once, neither of us argued.

We sat on the concrete in the dark, under the window where Channing was speaking to Zeke's evil twin brothers Hunter and Parker Brantley. We didn't call them the evil twins for nothing. If they knew we were here, we might be the next ones to die.

"Should we get out of here?" I whispered in Jackson's ear.

Before he could respond, Channing spoke from inside the building. "Yeah, you helped dispose of the bodies, but only because there was something in it for you. I'm done with doing that. I don't need your help anymore, so you're not fucking getting mine. You need to stop following us around before the same thing happens to you."

"Did you just threaten us?" Hunter's voice was amused, but dangerous. These guys were not to be fucked with. "Parker, did he just threaten us?"

"That's what it sounded like, yes," Parker agreed. He sounded less amused. "Listen here you little asswipe—"

Landon growled softly. I grabbed the back of his T-shirt to stop him from jumping up and storming into the building.

I got it, I really did. Channing was his boyfriend, his person. Although not official yet, I was their girlfriend, but I hadn't known either of them for anywhere near as long as they knew each other.

Threatening Channing was the same as threatening Landon. Honestly, I wanted to walk through the door and start tearing off some heads myself. Landon must be ready to land some punches. Or worse. But that might get him killed. I wasn't going to let that happen. He was my person. One of my guys. If anything bad happened to him… To any of them.

What even was this place? I glanced up and realised the window wasn't open, it was broken. Just another derelict building in the world. The front was covered in graffiti, but I couldn't tell if it was someone's name or words in German.

Somewhere in the back of my mind, I recognised that, if the building was empty, then no innocent lives would be lost if things went to shit.

More than they already had, that is.

"I can't let them hurt him," Landon moaned.

I had a sneaking suspicion the twins wouldn't hurt Channing. Not for very long anyway. They'd kill him and make him disappear like they had with all those bodies. The thought made my stomach twist all over again.

"We—" I started to say.

"Shhh," Jackson urged. "Someone is coming."

"They should be around here somewhere," that was Zeke's voice.

I was about to stand up and show myself when Asher spoke.

"Good. It's about time we dealt with those little shits."

I frowned. What the hell?

"Yeah," Zeke agreed. "Keep an eye out for Abbie and Landon. Fuck only knows where they are. I'm going to ring his neck when I find him."

"Probably fucking somewhere," Asher said lightly.

"Without Channing?" Zeke said. "Landon doesn't operate that way."

"Abbie has a way of changing things," Asher said.

I shook my head, trying to make sense of what they were saying. They knew Landon and Channing weren't together?

"Told you she'd be disruptive," Penn remarked.

"As if you're complaining," Tully scoffed.

"I never said I was," Penn said. "It doesn't mean I'm not right."

"Why are they all here?" Landon hissed. "I don't get it."

"Neither do I," Jackson said. "I think we should stay right where we are." His hand trembled lightly on my back.

"Sounds like we've got company," Hunter said. His voice was louder. He must have been standing right inside the window.

For a moment I thought he meant us, and ducked down lower.

"Brother dear," Parker said from the doorway. "I didn't realise we were having a party."

"You didn't?" Zeke said. He stepped inside the building and the others followed. "But I sent Channing with an invitation."

What the flying, cum-forsaken fuck? Zeke knew Channing was here?

Of course he did. He knew Channing and Landon weren't together. He'd only know that if he knew where Channing was.

My breath caught in my throat again. What else did he know?

"I didn't get a chance to deliver it," Channing said. "We were busy having a chat."

"We got the impression he doesn't like us," Hunter complained.

"Really? I wonder why that is?" Asher said. "For the record, I don't like you either."

"In case anyone was wondering, I hate your guts," Penn said. "Both of you. I'm still trying to decide which one of you is a bigger prick. So far it's a tie."

Fair enough, the twins *had* drugged him and left him where he could have drowned. He was probably itching to land a few punches himself.

"Is Landon with you?" Channing asked.

"He's out here," Tully said pausing on the doorstep. "With Abbie and Jackson."

Fuck. Of course Tully would know. He was a trained assassin. It was his job to notice anything and everything. What I didn't understand was, why didn't he keep his mouth shut? What the fuck was with everyone tonight?

"Shit," Zeke grunted.

One of the twins chuckled. "I guess they heard a bit then. I hope it was educational." Hunter stuck his head carefully out the broken window. Shame, all that broken glass could have given him a few nasty gashes.

Landon jumped up and swung, but Hunter pulled his head back before the punch connected.

"Hey, that's not nice. Zeke, call your hound off."

There was no holding Landon back now. The blue-haired bass player hurried into the building, hands curled into fists, body rigid with rage.

I looked at Jackson with wide eyes. What the hell should we do? A thousand thoughts whirled around my brain. I had no idea what the other guys knew about Channing. At this exact moment, I had no idea who to trust. Not even myself.

"It's okay, we've got you." Tully stepped away from the doorway and towards us. He reached out a hand. "Come on. It's all right."

I hesitated. I wanted to fall into his arms but I couldn't bring myself to move. Not toward him or away.

"Loveliness?" Tully crouched down in front of me. "I know this must be confusing." He put a hand on my arm.

I jerked away. "You think? What the hell is going on?"

"We'll explain everything," Tully assured me. "I'll take you back to the hotel."

I looked at him sideways, but slowly got to my feet, half an eye on the window in case something came flying out of it, like a bullet.

"The hell you are," I snapped. I wasn't going anywhere until I got an explanation for what the fuck was going on. Although... did I really want one? I thought I could trust these guys. Now...

"Sounds like your girlfriend isn't happy," one of the twins said. "We told her she should find some real men— Whoa."

That was followed by the cocking of a gun which echoed through the early morning like a crack.

"Shit." Jackson got to his feet and moved away from the window.

"You're not going to use that." I thought that was Hunter. He sounded wary. Maybe even scared. Good. It was about time he got some of his own back.

"Maybe I am," Zeke said evenly. "I've had enough of you to and your bullshit. Why don't you both take a seat?"

"See, loveliness, Zeke has it all under control," Tully said like he was talking to a wild animal. Or a child. "Everything is fine."

"No it fucking isn't," I said. "Not even slightly." I stepped past him and over to the doorway.

Hunter and Parker were sitting in two rickety old chairs in a corner, under the light of a single, naked bulb. Zeke had a gun in his hand. It was pointed at them. Where the fuck did he get that from?

Asher also had a gun, but he held it loosely, like he wasn't ready to use it immediately, if he had to. His body language said otherwise. I doubted anyone in the room was fooled.

Channing stood to one side near the wall, his hands in his back pockets.

Landon stared at him like he'd never seen him before.

Penn stood inside the door, his arms crossed over his chest until he saw me. He lowered them, but made no move towards me. "For what it's worth, I have no fucking idea what's going on either. Those two clowns left the room and Tully and I followed."

I flinched when Tully put a hand on my shoulder. "Zeke wanted the rest of us to stay out of it."

"Well we're in it now aren't we?" I said. "Does someone want to explain what the fuck is going on?"

"In a minute," Zeke said, his gaze unwavering. He shoved Hunter forward in his chair, making him hunch over. He patted him, presumably looking for a gun.

He did the same to Parker before he pulled his brother's phone out of his back pocket. "It's time Reuben and I had a little chat." He pressed Parker against the back of his seat and stepped away. The gun unmoving in one hand, he pressed the phone screen with the other. "Passcode," he snapped.

"That's private—" Parker started to say. He stopped when he found the nozzle of the gun pressed against his forehead. "Six, nine, six, nine."

Zeke snorted. "Of course it is. Very creative of you."

Any other time, someone would have joked that Zeke's pass code would be the same thing. But no one was joking now.

Zeke's thumb slid across the screen, lighting it up. "It should be about three o'clock in the afternoon in Australia. Reuben has probably just finished torturing someone for the day."

I wasn't sure if he was joking or not, but he was the one with a gun to his brother's head. At this point, anything was possible.

Parker's phone made an old-fashioned ringing sound. The video call connected a minute or so later.

"You're not Parker," Reuben remarked.

From where I stood, I only made out part of the oldest Brantley brother's face. I didn't need to see the irritation, I heard it. He wasn't getting any sympathy from me. Reuben deserved a gun to his head as much as the twins did. Maybe more.

"No shit," Zeke said. "Don't worry, he's right here. He and Hunter are doing their best not to shit their pants."

"I'm not gonna shit my pants," Hunter said. He looked like he was going to say something else when Zeke turned the gun on him. "Okay, I might pee myself a little."

"How about you shut up?" Asher suggested, his

tone dangerously polite. "It's early morning and I haven't had coffee yet."

"Did you want something?" Reuben asked as though he was bored with the conversation already.

"No, just letting you know I'm going to kill Hunter and Parker," Zeke said cheerfully.

2

ABBIE

"No, you won't," Reuben said.

"You think not?" Zeke asked. "Is this where you say I don't have it in me to kill my brothers? Because I think you're underestimating how pissed off I am."

I'd seen him angry before, but right now he burned with cold rage. Icy, terrifyingly calm. I had absolutely no doubt in my mind he would blow the twins brains out and not regret it.

I caught Asher's expression in the corner of my eye. It matched Zeke's. They had come here to do one thing and that was deal with Hunter and Parker once and for all. I didn't know where Channing fit into all of this, but it seemed unlikely all of us would leave this room alive.

"I'm sure you're perfectly capable of killing them,"

Reuben said. "You might even be doing me a favour."

"What the fuck?" Hunter whispered. He fell silent again at a look from Asher.

"I think I'd be doing a lot of people a favour," Zeke said. "Especially their girlfriend, Lila Bell."

The silence that came from the other end of the phone suggested that was news to Reuben. Full points to Zeke for dropping that little bombshell at the right time.

"Fucking hell," Parker muttered. "You might as well kill us. If you don't, he will."

"As tempting as that is," Reuben said finally, his tone clipped irritation, "we have more important matters to deal with."

Zeke's eyes narrowed. "If you're trying to—"

Reuben interrupted. "One of my contacts has informed me Dante Fiorelli is planning to make a move against you once you reach American soil. All three of you. And anyone you're with."

I almost felt him trying to look down the phone to see who else was in the room and resisted the urge to poke my tongue out at him. It was a good idea not to provoke Reuben Brantley. Or any of them really. Zeke was the one with a gun in his hand.

Zeke growled. "What part of me not being

involved with your business does this asshole not get?"

"The bit where we share a last name," Reuben said. "And the bit where the twins work for me." By the sound of it, that arrangement might come to an end shortly if what Zeke said about Lila Bell was true. Which, according to the twins, it was. I remember Zeke and Asher describing the Bell family as the worst of the worst, but so far they were the only ones who hadn't given us any trouble.

That I knew of.

Yet.

"All the more reason I should dispose of these two now," Zeke said. "If the Fiorellis see I'm not on your side, they might leave me the fuck alone."

"They still won't," Reuben said. "Dante is determined to eradicate all of us. As irritating as they might be, you need the twins to help you when they come after you."

"Well, that's fucking awesome," Penn said sarcastically. "I love it when we get involved in Reuben's shit. Maybe we don't go to America."

"If they don't come after us there, they'll try again in Australia," Zeke said. "We've already proven we can take care of ourselves and deal with whatever shit they throw at us. We can do it again."

"Yes, we can," Asher agreed. "What will you be doing in the meantime, Reuben? You must know by now my brother has sided with the Bells?"

"I'm aware of that," Reuben said coldly. "I'm working on an alliance between the three families to keep the Fiorellis at bay. In the meantime, the twins are at your disposal to keep you from getting killed."

"Does that mean we don't get to dispose of them?" Asher complained.

"I still haven't ruled that out," Zeke said. He was silent for a moment or two. "I'll do you a deal, Reuben. I won't kill the twins on two conditions."

"He accepts," Hunter said immediately.

"What are those conditions?" Reuben asked evenly. Apparently he wasn't as eager to accept the offer as his brother. Business before blood. What a charming family.

"First, that they never try to kill or injure me or anyone I care about," Zeke said. "Second, you stop wanting me to come back to the family. For good. Leave me alone to live my life. I know you don't want either of them dead. They're too useful to you."

"We really are," Parker said. "Very useful. Much more useful than Zeke." He flinched away from Asher's gun. "No offence or anything. Zeke doesn't *want* to be useful to the family."

"No I don't," Zeke agreed. "So, do we have a deal?"

Reuben sighed heavily. "Fine. If you want to spend the rest of your life travelling around the world playing music, then do it. You were never much use to the family anyway."

Zeke rolled his eyes. "I'll take that as a compliment."

"Hey, I just realised something," Hunter said. "Reuben can't ask us to kill each other." He offered Parker a high-five.

"I said people I care about," Zeke said.

"We know you care about us." Parker raised his hand, but instead of accepting the high-five, he eyed Hunter. "Would you do it if he asked you to?"

"Of course not," Hunter said. "My point is that he can't ask us to, that's all." He lowered his hand.

"I can still ask," Reuben said darkly. "Only if you stop being useful."

"Most. Dysfunctional. Family. Ever," Penn said.

"Ever?" Tully echoed. "It's a pretty high bar around here." He had killed his own adopted father in self-defence after all.

Landon's mother was an addict who left him alone him often as a child. Asher's family was into the same shit as the Brantleys. Penn's pressured him mercilessly to succeed. From what I gathered, Channing's family was as bad. They must have been terrible for him to end up a killer.

Yeah, the bar was certainly high.

Penn shrugged. "I stand by what I said."

"Fair enough." Tully nodded slowly.

"I thought so," Penn agreed.

"Can we go now?" Hunter asked. "We have a flight in a few hours, don't we?" He eyed the gun which was still aimed at his head.

Zeke lowered it reluctantly. "I guess so." He looked like he would prefer to poke out his own eyeballs than be on the same flight with the evil twins. Honestly, the only people in the room who didn't share that sentiment were the twins themselves, I assumed. They seemed to enjoy travelling together. Two toxic peas in a pod.

"Can I have my phone back?" Parker raised his hands to either side and rose up from the chair. He kept his eyes on Zeke and Asher.

Yeah, I would too. Neither of them looked like they'd ruled out the idea of killing the twins. Or at least, they hadn't dampened the desire to do it completely.

"Wait," I found myself saying. "Before you hang up the phone, I have another condition of these two walking out of here alive."

Nine sets of eyes turned to look at me.

Asher used his gun to wave Parker back down into his seat.

Both twins eyed me nervously.

That shouldn't have turned me on, but it did. Their fear and the fact the guys took me seriously in this. None of them laughed me off, told me to be quiet or anything like that. They were all ready to hear whatever I had to say. Yeah, attentiveness in a tense situation was hot.

"What is it, sweetheart?" Zeke asked, no hint of condescension in his tone..

"Do enlighten us," Reuben said dryly. Okay, you can't impress everyone.

"They get to walk out of here with their brains inside their heads if they leave us alone after whatever happens in America," I said. "You said you accept that Zeke isn't coming back to the family, but I don't want these two following us around, drugging us, kidnapping us, threatening us, or anything like that."

"Abbie makes a good point," Zeke said. "Unless we need their help with some other shit you bring down on us, then they stay away from us. Especially from Abbie." He jerked his head in my direction.

"And me," Penn said. "I haven't ruled out killing them at a later date."

"Condition from me," Reuben said. "You don't kill them at a later date. None of you. Otherwise, I agree to your terms. Is there anything else?"

"Can you not kill my brother?" Asher asked. "Or any of my family?"

I caught a glimpse of Reuben's expression on the screen, but I couldn't figure out the reason for it. He looked uncomfortable. Cagier than usual.

"I have no intention of killing any member of the DiMarco family," Reuben said. "Not even Dane."

"Excellent," Asher said lightly. "Then it seems like we have a deal." He lowered his gun fully and stepped away from the twins.

"Now we're gonna have to find something else to do for fun," Parker quipped. He grinned and rose again, hands still in the air.

"Get a hobby," Zeke said. He too lowered his gun and handed Parker back his phone. "Take up knitting or some shit." He didn't look like he cared, as long as it was as far from him as possible.

Hunter laughed and stood just behind Parker. "Let's deal with the Fiorelli family first, shall we? Hey, Channing, good news. We won't have to get any help from you after all." He moved past him and clapped the saxophonist on the shoulder. "Looks like you're off the hook. On the other hand, you're going to have to deal with dead bodies by yourself from now on."

Channing jerked away. "Fuck off."

"Now, now, that's not very nice," Parker scolded.

"Don't make me change my mind," Zeke growled.

"You can't change your mind, we have a deal," Hunter said. "And in case you hadn't noticed, that also means Channing can't kill us. Isn't that awesome?"

Channing bared his teeth at him.

My gaze settled on Landon, who hadn't taken his eyes off his boyfriend the entire time. He still looked scared and confused. Pretty much how I felt.

"I hate to go all manager on you," Jackson said, "but we should get back to the hotel. We also have a flight to get ready for and a shit load of explaining to do."

"Yeah, we do," Zeke agreed. "Some of us more than others."

"Some a lot more than others," Penn said, waving a hand in Channing's direction. "Right now the only thing I've got is that these two assholes a walking away scot-free, and Zeke doesn't have to worry about his family anymore. Apart from that, I don't know what the fuck is going on."

"Me either," I admitted. I caught a smile on Zeke's face and frowned. "What?"

"I just realised you're wearing my shirt," he said. "You look adorable."

I glanced down at myself. His T-shirt fell almost to my knees like a dress. My track pants peeked out from underneath. I shrugged. "I grabbed whatever I could find. And before you ask, yes, I am wearing underwear."

"There goes that fantasy," Hunter complained as he slipped out the door behind Parker.

I made a face. The only thing I wanted to do with either of their cocks was punch them. Or pull them off and shove them down their throats.

A hand slipped into mine and I turned to see Tully.

"Are you okay, loveliness?" he asked softly.

"Not really," I said. Far from it. It was nice to get the twins off our backs, but now we were facing a potential attack in another country and the reality that Channing wasn't the person any of us thought he was.

Worse than that, the possibility Zeke and Asher knew what he was doing all along.

3

CHANNNIG

LANDON LOOKED at me like I kicked his puppy.

That was a dumb analogy, he'd never had a puppy. His mother wouldn't let him have one. And neither would any of his foster parents. Honestly, he spent most of the time looking after his useless fucking mother, trying to make excuses for the bitch, or trying to stay out of trouble. From what he told me, it only took a sniff of anything bad for a foster family to decide it was time for him to move on.

I would never understand why no one adopted him. He's the best guy I know.

And right now the expression on his face was breaking my heart.

"Sweetie—" I held my hand out to him, tentative but hoping he'd take it.

"Did you really do those things?" he asked in a hushed whisper. He didn't take my hand. Instead, he stepped over closer to Abbie and Tully, who sat on the end of one bed.

Zeke and Asher sat on another, while Penn and Jackson leaned against the walls.

The sun had risen. The glow slanted through a gap in the curtains, illuminating the room.

"Did you know about it?" Abbie asked Zeke and Asher. She looked tired and confused. Her blonde hair stuck up here and there, untamed and adorable. Now wasn't the time for me to tell her that. Later, when she understood.

Zeke shrugged. "I had my suspicions, but I wasn't sure until tonight. Um, this morning."

I expected him to look pissed off, but he didn't. Why should he? I'd only killed people who deserved it. No one innocent. Nothing he wouldn't have done, given the chance. Me—I had the chances and took them.

Landon still hadn't taken his eyes off me.

I took a deep breath and prepared to tell him everything, and have him hate me for it. That was the worst part. I didn't regret anything I did, except working with the evil twins, but if Landon didn't love me anymore, then it was all for nothing.

"Yes, I did all those things," I said simply. What more was there to say?

Abbie put an arm around Landon when he groaned.

"Why?" she asked.

Zeke was right, she looked adorable in his shirt. And out of it. Everything about her was the image of the perfect woman. Her face, her voice, her figure, the way she tasted. The way she bucked against my mouth when I licked her clit and made her come. Even the way she growled at me when I edged her. She loved it and she knew it.

I set my mouth in a line. "When Zeke told me about Jonah, I lost it," I said. "Not in an out-of-control kind of way, but I got angry. You're my family. Your enemies are my enemies. I tracked him down and... I don't know what I intended to do. Maybe just beat him up, or warn him off. The next thing I knew, I had my hands around his neck and he was dead. And it felt fucking good to know he couldn't hurt any of you again." It really had. Guys like him got off on hurting people, and they got paid for it. They were low life pieces of shit. They deserved a slower, more painful death than I gave.

I glanced down at the floor, then back up again. "I know that's all kinds of fucked up." It was, but I still didn't flinch from what I did. I owned every moment.

Penn snorted. "You think? That's at least seventeen thousand kinds of fucked up. You could have ended up dead yourself."

"But I didn't," I said even. "I got rid of a threat and it felt good." My gaze swung over to Asher. "Like it felt good to shoot that guy in Perth."

Asher gave an unapologetic half shrug. "Not gonna lie, it did feel good."

I moved my gaze to Tully. "I know it didn't feel good to kill Xavier Lang, but you did what you had to do to protect yourself and us."

"I didn't hunt him down," Tully pointed out. "But you're right. Sometimes you have to do bad shit to bad people to keep better people safe."

I noticed he didn't say, 'good people,' when he looked at me, but he didn't seem to be condemning me either.

I nodded and turned my gaze back to Landon and Abbie.

"When I realised what I did, I didn't want to throw Jonah in a shallow grave or into the harbour. I didn't have time to do either of those things anyway. And no shovel."

"So you grabbed a cardboard box, put his head

inside it and put him outside Zeke's door?" Abbie asked.

"Basically, yes," I agreed. "I'm sorry I freaked you out, that was never my intention." I was wrong, I had some regrets. That was one of them. I hadn't meant to scare her, just let her know someone was looking out for her. For all of my family.

Abbie looked sceptical. "What about the rest of them?" She frowned and asked, "When Asher and Zeke were confronting Reuben over having me kidnapped the first time, Landon said you had something to take care of. Was it Vance?"

Landon's eyes were huge and his mouth popped open. I could see thoughts turning in his mind, knowing the hints were there, but he hadn't seen them. Of course, he hadn't known to look.

"Yes, it was," I admitted. "I saw how hurt you were and… I'd already fallen for you. I couldn't stand seeing you hurt like that. So I went to confront him too."

"When we went souvenir shopping in Melbourne," Landon said slowly. "You said you had a surprise for me. Something you wanted to organise."

Penn snapped his fingers. "That's right, I remember thinking Channing bought a lot less shit than Landon did. You usually buy about the same amount of crap."

I couldn't deny it, so I nodded. "I also bought a cute hat for Landon. But yeah, I might have dropped in on Calista Rossi. Then I had to stash her quickly before we moved on to Adelaide. One of the staff must have seen me with the suitcase, that was why they left it outside the hotel room."

"And Poppy Newton?" Jackson asked.

"I was going to the toilet and bumped into her doing the same," I said. "She started asking me all sorts of questions about Abbie and being nasty. I didn't plan to do anything to her, but she kept coming at me and coming at me. In the end, I shoved her into the wall and she hit her head. I don't regret doing that either." She was a pain in Abbie's ass for years. And tons of other celebrities. If I hadn't ended her, someone else would have. I did a lot of people a favour ridding the world of that bloodsucking bitch. Unfortunately, someone else would take her place. They always did.

"Did you have anything to do with Pete's death?" Abbie asked.

"Same story," I said. "I went to the toilet and so did he. He didn't recognise me, but I tripped him over. He struck his head on the sink and I left him there like that. I didn't know he was dead until you told me."

"I can't believe…" Landon said, his eyes glazed.

Okay, here it came. He hated my guts. Never wanted to see me again. If that was the case, I would be the one to quit the band. I wasn't going to force him out of it. What was I thinking? After everything I told them, they'd probably turn me in to the police. The band would be the least of my trouble. This was going to cause a shitstorm for everyone. Fuck, I hadn't meant to…

"I can't believe," he started again, "that you would do all that and not tell me about it. And not ask for my help."

I blinked.

Okay, that was *not* what I expected to hear.

"You wanted to help?" I asked. Was I hearing things? Yeah, I'd finally lost my last marble.

His mouth open and closed a couple of times. "I can't exactly say I *wanted* to, but you're my person and everything you did was to protect us. It was like one of the twins said, it was your love letter to us."

"You're not mad at me?" I asked tentatively. "For killing people?"

He sucked in a breath. "It's going to take some time for me to get used to the idea that you did what you did, but I'm upset you didn't take me along with you to do these things. I know I'm not the strongest guy in the world, but I promised a long time ago that I would be by your side always. No matter what we're doing."

All right, had someone flipped the planet upside down? None of them were looking angrily at me. Zeke, Asher and Tully all looked like they understood. Jackson looked a bit freaked out. Penn looked somewhere between bored and amused.

And Abbie— Abbie looked aroused. To be fair, she usually was. She had a bigger appetite for sex than any woman I ever met. Or man for that matter.

"If this is where you say you'll take Landon along the next time," Zeke said slowly but firmly, "then this is where I say it needs to stop. I appreciate you wanting to take care of our problems, I really do. The rest of us do too, but sooner or later you're going to get caught and then we're all fucked. Okay?"

"Okay," I agreed.

"Who's left anyway?" Asher asked. "Like the evil twins said, you can't kill them." He glanced over to Abbie. "You don't have any more enemies do you?"

"Not now Penn and I are getting along," she agreed, a smile on the corners of her gorgeous mouth.

Penn snorted. "No fucking way Channing could kill me anyway. I'm bigger than him and we all know I'm faster than him." He puffed his chest out, full of self importance.

Not gonna lie, I was still annoyed he beat me in the foot race around the stadium in Munich. We hadn't had a chance for a rematch, but I planned to kick his ass next time. Especially now I apparently wasn't out of the band. I knew these people were the best.

"I don't want to kill you," I told him, "but I'm going to beat you next time we race."

"You talk a big game," Penn said, "but you only get to crow after you win."

"You guys are absolutely nuts." Jackson scrubbed a hand over his face. "Channing killed five people and you're talking about a foot race."

My heart thudded in my chest. "Are you going to go to the police? Or to Levi?"

"I didn't tell them about Asher or Tully, did I?" Jackson asked. "No, I'm not going to tell the police. Besides, I helped you clean up one of those heads, didn't I? I witnessed what Asher did in Perth. I'm in this as deep as you guys are. But that doesn't mean you're not absolutely nuts."

"But we're your nuts," Asher said. He frowned

when he realised what he'd said. "I mean, we're not your nuts. Your nuts are your nuts, but we're—"

"We get it, babe." Zeke leaned to rest his cheek against Asher's shoulder. "Jackson is stuck with us, because he knows all the shit we did."

"Exactly," Asher said cheerfully. "Manager, friend, accomplice."

Jackson groaned.

"Are you going to tell Levi?" Abbie asked.

Jackson looked over at her, a pained expression on his face. "Levi knows pretty much everything there is to know about you guys. None of this will surprise him. And I hate to say it, but at the end of the day, you guys make him a lot of money. If he went to the police, there's no way in hell we would keep this from going public. Wolf Venom would implode. White Wolf Records would implode and take Onyx Riot with it."

He sighed out pursed lips. "And at the end of the day, I can't exactly say…" He chose his words carefully. "Jonah would have killed Abbie if it wasn't for Zeke. Pete was stalking her. Vance was an asshole who used her—"

"How to say you approve of what Channing did without saying you approve of what Channing did," Penn said sardonically.

"I wouldn't say I *approve*," Jackson said. "Just that I understand. But I would prefer if it didn't happen again. Can we agree to that?" He turned his denim blue eyes to me. He looked tired, more so than usual.

"Yes, I can agree," I said. "I'm done." It wasn't like I was some kind of psychopath who got joy out of killing people. Not precisely.

I stepped over to Landon and held out my hand. I looked him right in the eyes and silently begged him to take it. He was right, I should have taken him along. I should have trusted that he would understand and keep his mouth shut. Sometimes I forgot how strong he really was. On the surface, it seemed like he was just about to come apart, but under that he was the toughest person I knew. Tougher than me.

He reached out with calloused fingers and curled them around mine and I let out a breath of relief.

"Are we good?" I asked as I pulled him towards me.

I got my answer when he wound his arms around my neck and kissed my mouth.

"That leaves another question," Zeke said. He turned and pointed at me. "Don't think I haven't forgotten about your involvement with the twins."

Everyone's eyes turned to me.

4

ABBIE

"WELCOME to another episode of confessions from Wolf Venom," Asher said. His tone was cheerful but his eyes were as curious as everyone else's.

"For the record, I have nothing to confess," Penn said. "What you see is what you get." He shot me a heated look, clearly suggesting he meant that literally.

As if I wasn't turned on enough right now.

Yeah, I also have a confession. It was all kinds of fucked up to be aroused by what Channing did, but I was. What he did, he did because he loved me and Landon. It was the most morbid romantic gesture I'd ever had, but I couldn't deny my life was easier without the people he'd killed.

Like I said, I knew that was fucked up, but there

was a reason I fit in with these guys. We were all about each other, no matter what. Nothing and no one was going to come between us.

"Which brings us back to Channing working with the twins," Zeke said reluctantly. "I need to know what you told them."

Channing closed his eyes and leaned into me and Landon.

"I'm sorry. I shouldn't have—" he started.

"That doesn't matter now," Zeke interrupted. "What did you tell them?"

"Nothing they didn't already know," Channing said. "Or nothing they couldn't find out from other sources. I made it sound like it was inside information. You didn't think I'd really tell them shit, did you?"

Zeke looked back at him, unflinching. "There's something about disposing of bodies together that tends to bond people. Not to mention, there's something about blackmail that makes people do things they would otherwise not. So, I'd be pissed if you had, but not surprised."

"I'd be surprised," Landon said. "I know Channing wouldn't betray us. Would you Chan?"

"Hell no," Channing agreed. He gave Zeke a dark look for suggesting he would.

Zeke was as unmoved as ever. "Does anyone have anything else they'd like to admit, confess, get off their chest?" He spread his hands out to take us all in.

"Jackson, if you're going to admit your undying love for Abbie, Levi or any of us, here's your chance," Asher said.

Jackson glanced sideways at me, but instead of admitting anything, he rolled his eyes.

"I admit my undying love for coffee, which I'd love a cup of right now, and travelling around the world managing bands." He was almost convincing. "There is something you should know," he added. He looked like he'd prefer to have a tooth pulled than say what he was about to say.

Almost as though we read each other's minds, all of us crossed our arms over our chests.

"Okay, out with it," Asher said. He gave me a quick look as if to say, 'here it comes, he's about to admit he's head over heels for you.'

Jackson grimaced. "Believe it or not, Levi offered me a job behind a desk."

Zeke dropped his arms to his sides and gaped. "Come again?"

"We're all going to need a bunch of orgasms after this bullshit," Penn muttered.

Without taking his eyes off Jackson, Asher

offered Penn a high five.

Penn accepted and their palms slapped together lightly.

Zeke gave them the side eye, then looked back at Jackson. "Since when, and why didn't I know about it?"

"Since Levi wants to expand White Wolf Records," Jackson said. "Including incorporating Onyx Riot into the business." He nodded towards me, since I was previously signed with the label.

"He wants me to sit in an office all day long and push paper around. That phone call you overheard while you were in the shower—"

Now all eyes turned to me. "I was trying not to listen," I protested.

Jackson offered a half smile, like he knew I wouldn't have eavesdropped on purpose.

"That was a reporter asking when I'd be taking up the job and who would be replacing me. When I said I wasn't, they asked if I had a relationship with Abbie and if that was the reason I wanted to stay with you guys. I'd been fielding calls like that all day and had enough by then."

He scrubbed a hand across his face. "Maybe I should take Levi up on his offer. I'm sure he can find someone else—"

"Are you fucking kidding?" Asher asked, looking horrified. "Who else would put up with our bullshit? Who else would hear what you've heard this morning and not freak out?"

"Everyone but us eight," I said, giving Jackson a, 'don't you fucking dare leave us,' look. "Now I know what it was about, I wish I'd made you tell me. I would have talked you out of it." I probably would have blown him into staying. I still might.

He gestured with a brief wave of his hand. "At the time, you did ask if I was all right. I could have come out with it then, but we all had enough on our plates. If I knew you were so... worried about me, I would have come forward sooner."

He glanced down at the floor and sighed heavily. "I'm sorry my secrets aren't as interesting as Channing's." Yeah, he was one of us all right, or we were rubbing off on him. His sense of humour was as bad as ours.

"No one feels bad they aren't," Zeke said. "Levi really thought he could pry you away from us?"

"Either Levi doesn't know you as well as we thought, or he doesn't know us," Asher said. "They would have to pry our manager out of our cold, dead fingers. Unless you *wanted* to leave. But please don't."

"Yeah, what Asher said," Penn said. "No other manager would put up with Asher the way you do."

With all the maturity of a professional drummer in his mid-twenties, Asher stuck out his tongue at Penn.

Penn sneered at him. "No one else would put up with me either, okay dickhead?"

"You two are doing a good job of illustrating why we need Jackson," Zeke said. "On the other hand, if you keep being assholes like that, he might be tempted to walk away from us."

"Is this where we all rush at Jackson and give him a group hug?" Landon asked.

"I think it might be," I agreed.

Jackson held up his hands. "That's not necessary—"

Of course, we ignored him, rushed at him and gathered around for a group hug. After a moment, he gave up and hugged us back.

I totally didn't miss the way his hand found its way to my ass. Or mine to his.

"You know I might not always be able to go on tour with you," he said with what breath he could get out past our squeezes. "Blazing Violet needs me too. And Abbie."

"We can share," Asher said. "As long as you

remember you really belong to us." He stepped back and rubbed his hands together like he was some evil character from an animated movie.

"If that doesn't make Jackson rethink working with us, nothing will," Tully said dryly.

"Nah, he likes our special brand of silly," Asher said. "Don't you Jackson?"

Jackson made a face in response. "It's been noted a couple of times we have a flight to prepare for. I'm also going to need to speak to Levi." He ran a hand over his hair. "We're going to need additional security."

Zeke nodded. "I'll sit down with you and discuss the travel itinerary. Figure out where we need extra people and extra vigilance. Places we're more likely to come under attack and places they'll expect us to be complacent."

"Does this mean we'll be on house arrest for the rest of the tour?" Penn groaned.

"No," Zeke shook his head. "I'd prefer to draw them out and deal with them. To do that, we're going to have to act as normal as possible." When Asher opened his mouth to say something, he quickly added, "I said as normal as *possible*, not actually normal. I don't think normal is realistic for any of us."

"I hope not," Asher said. "That would suck. I don't want to be normal and boring."

"You could never be boring, babe," Zeke assured him.

"I second that," I said. "None of us are boring."

"But some of us are more interesting than others," Penn said, without a hint of modesty.

"Yes, me," Tully said. Also with no modesty.

The guys all stepped back, leaving me with my arm still around Jackson.

"How did the press know?" I asked. They always seemed able to worm their way into any situation to get information. They were nothing if not as intrusive as fuck.

"Probably someone at the label told them," Jackson said. "It's not exactly a state secret. Most of the other managers have ended up behind a desk and I've been there longer than a lot of them. It might have been nothing more than a lucky guess."

"Being stuck behind a fucking desk sounds like the worst kind of torture," Penn said.

"Exactly my point," Jackson said. "And what I've been telling him all this time. I'd rather deal with disembodied heads than paperwork."

"What can I say?" Asher said. "You have your priorities in order, that's for sure."

"I'd rather deal with neither of those things," I said.

"If we don't start getting ready, we're going to be dealing with missing our flight," Tully pointed out.

"New York cheesecake, here we come," Landon said happily.

I closed my eyes and groaned. "Oh my god, that sounds so good right now." It seemed like days since Landon and I found the hotel's chef and front desk staff fucking in the kitchen. I'd hoped to find pastries instead. I'd lost my appetite hearing what Channing did, but now Landon mentioned cheesecake, it came back with a vengeance.

"We can eat in the airport," Zeke said. He was apologetic, but it was all aimed at me, along with a soft, loving look, which I returned.

"I'm okay with that," I said. "I'd like to get the heck out of Europe."

"That seems to be a theme with us," Asher said. "Come in with a blaze of glory and go out running for our lives."

"It's a theme I'd like to stop," Zeke said. "I'm okay with a blaze of glory stuff but not the rest of it."

"I'm seriously considering the wisdom of going to North America," Jackson said. "The sensible thing might be to organise a private jet and drop off the grid. Let your family deal with the Fiorellis, Bell family, and whoever the hell else." He held up a hand. "I know you want to finish the tour, but is it worth dying for?"

"No," Zeke said. "But we're not going to die. We're going to deal with whatever they throw at us. You can come with us or you can go home and sit in an office. Or go and lie on a beach and have a few cocktails. You deserve a break. But we *are* going to finish this tour and we're going to do it in style and without dying. I can't claim we won't break a sweat."

"I guarantee I'll break a sweat," Penn said. He gave me a look that sent heat right to my clit.

I looked back at him and grinned. Oh yeah, I'd be happy to work up a sweat with him any day. And lots and lots of orgasms.

"I'm not going home," Jackson said firmly, but with a sigh. "Whatever happens, we'll deal with it together."

"If you'd like, I can field your calls for you," Penn said. "I'm good at telling those bloodsucking vultures from the press to fuck off. In fact, it would be a pleasure."

"Thank you for the offer," Jackson said graciously. "I'll keep it in mind."

5

ABBIE

"ARE YOU OKAY?" I asked Landon the first chance we got to speak alone together.

All Zeke gave us time for was to finish throwing our belongings into suitcases and make ourselves look more or less presentable. None of that took long, but it was still a mad scramble. We bumped into each other and almost tripped over suitcases several times. The mood was light but with an edge that it might change at any moment.

Judging by the looks, the covert glances, we were all trying to get our heads around what Channing did. You couldn't drop a bomb and not expect a bang.

"Yeah." Landon pressed the palm of his hand against mine and we laced our fingers together. "I feel like I should have known somehow. We all practically live together before the tour, and we're in each other's pockets when we're on tour. No one can go to the toilet without everyone knowing. But he went off and killed people and none of us had a clue."

"Love is blind?" I suggested. "Sometimes we don't see what's right in front of our faces." I hadn't seen what Vance was up to until after I married the guy. I had no clue he didn't care about me, even though it was as obvious as fuck. He might as well have walked around with a red flag in his hand, or on his forehead.

"I'm sorry," he said softly. "I didn't mean to remind you of him. But... he can't bother you anymore."

I snorted softly. "Thanks to Channing."

"You're welcome," Channing said.

I hadn't known he walked up behind me until he spoke. I startled and looked over my shoulder. Part of me thought I should be scared of him, knowing what he did, what he was capable of. But I wasn't. He was still the same Channing, buff, hot, with an edge of mystery. He loved me enough to kill for me. What could be more romantic?

"Sorry, didn't mean to scare you." He put tentative

hands on my shoulders, as though he wasn't sure if I would welcome his touch. When I didn't tell him to stop, he started to massage lightly, strong fingers ironing out tight knots.

"You didn't," I said quickly.

"Are you sure?" he asked. "Both of you. It's not every day you learn your boyfriend killed people."

"I was standing right there in Perth when Asher killed that guy right in front of us," I pointed out. "I've known right from the start you guys were into all sorts of shit. You haven't seen me running away, have you?"

"No, but I have seen you freaking out over finding a head," Channing said. "After the first time, it seemed like the right thing to do, to keep doing that. So you knew someone was looking out for you. Even though you thought it was Pete." His fingers tightened on my shoulders.

"At least we know it's not a crazed fan," I said.

His fingers loosened and he went back to messaging. "Not crazed, no. I'm definitely a fan."

He stopped and turned me around to face him. He leaned in to slant his mouth over mine and kissed me, softly but putting all of his feelings into it. If I had any doubt of his intentions, he washed them all away.

He broke off and curled his fingers in the front of Landon's shirt. He pulled him over to him and kissed him too.

Landon wound his arms around Channing's neck and kissed him like he was starving.

"Are you guys ready?" Zeke called out like a bucket of ice cold water dumped on a fire.

The guys reluctantly broke off and made a face at Zeke.

"Yeah," Channing said. He kissed Landon again quickly and made to step away.

Before he could, Landon held him there and said, "I love you." He let him go and placed a hand on the back of my head, under my hair. "I love you," he said, his breath brushing my cheek.

"I love you too," I said. I thought about saying it to Channing, but the time wasn't quite right. Not yet. I had to get my head around everything first. That would take me at least a day or two.

"Let's get our stuff and get out of here," Channing said.

I suspected he caught my vibe. We both knew we cared about each other, but putting it into words wasn't something either of us could do right now. The time would come soon enough, as long as we didn't die.

In spite of Zeke's assurances, I wasn't going to assume anything.

"As long as you promise we're not going to find any more heads," I said. "Unless they are attached to living people." There were twelve heads in the room I was pretty fond of, on shoulders and in pants. Thirteen if I counted my own.

"If we find any more disembodied heads, it wasn't because of me," Channing assured me. "I can't guarantee I won't kill anyone in the defence of my family. You guys I mean, not my biological family."

"That bad?" I asked.

"I'll tell you about them later." He crouched to zip up his suitcase and pull the handle out.

"Okay," I said softly. He'd tell me when he was ready. From what I gathered, they were homophobic. People like that didn't deserve a guy like him.

I grabbed the handle of my own suitcase and wheeled it toward the door. "Can I ask you something?" I asked.

"Sure," he said. "Now you know what I did, I'm mostly an open book."

"When Tully was talking about... What you did, he said it was rough. You asked him what he meant by that."

Channing nodded. "A guy has to have some pride in his work, right?"

Landon and I both made a face at him.

He chuckled. "No, I was curious how he knew. I mean, it's not like I have that much experience at this."

"Are you sure about that?" I asked teasingly. At least, I *thought* I was teasing. Was that something I should tease him about?

Yes, I decided, it was. Firstly, I wanted to know the answer to that question and secondly, we wouldn't be us if we didn't all have morbid senses of humour.

Channing gave me a lopsided smile. "I solemnly swear I've only killed five people." He stopped for a moment and frowned in thought. "Yeah, five. I had to count to be sure. Wouldn't want to under exaggerate."

"Or over exaggerate," Landon said. He looked like he hoped five was an over exaggeration.

"Or that," Channing agreed. He seemed lighter now, happier. Compared to how he was before anyway. Considering what he had off his chest, it was no wonder.

"Hey, Asher," Penn said, "how many people have you killed?"

Asher stopped with his hand on the door handle. "I don't know." He shrugged.

"You don't know?" I blinked at him a couple of times. Holy shit.

A slow smile crept onto his face. "Less than Channing. I'm guessing, more than Penn, Landon or Abbie."

"Fewer than me," Tully said softly.

"I haven't killed anyone," Landon said. "Just a few spiders."

"Me either," I said. Did I really need to say that? I think they probably all knew that already. Before I met them, I felt bad if I stood on an ant. Now, this whole conversation didn't even bother me as much as it probably should. Yeah, I definitely changed.

"I pissed off a few people, but I've never killed them," Penn said.

"That sounds accurate," Zeke said. He waved at Asher to open the door.

"You don't think we're going to leave without you telling us how many people you've killed, do you?" Penn asked Zeke.

"A guy is entitled to keep some things a mystery," Zeke said. "Come on, let's go."

"Either it's a shit load, or its none," Penn said. "If it's a shit load, they weigh on your mind. If it's none, it's going to fuck with your reputation for being a badass."

"If we don't leave here soon, it will be more than zero either way," Zeke growled. "I'm sure the twins have time to dispose of you before they follow us."

Penn held up the hand that wasn't curled around his suitcase handle, in surrender. "Fine, don't tell us. You're a bigger spoilsport than Jackson."

"Don't you forget it," Zeke said. The set of his mouth was grim. However many was, it was definitely a non-zero number.

Honestly, I didn't want to know. Not right now anyway. I was one thousand percent certain he wouldn't have done it if he didn't have to.

Asher looked at us over his shoulder. "Are we good? Because once we step out the door, we have to stop talking about killing people and shit like that. Because, you know we're in a hotel in Frankfurt and there are other people here."

"I'm good," I said. "Maybe we could talk about something else for a while. Like puppies."

"I like puppies," Zeke said.

"Does anyone *not* like puppies?" Penn asked. "I have the hardest heart of all of us and I like puppies. Until they piss on your leg."

"Has that happened often?" Asher asked curiously.

"I can't say it has," Penn admitted. "But enough to know I don't like it."

"Fair enough." Asher nodded. He finally turned the door handle and opened the door. He peered out one way, then the other. "It looks more or less safe."

"Okay, everyone, keep your eyes open in case Reuben's intel was wrong," Zeke said. "It wouldn't be the first time someone fed someone else false information so they get complacent." His eyes scanned the group.

As soon as he said it, I realised he was right. That was exactly what happened, at least for me. It hadn't occurred to me we might come under attack before we left Frankfurt. My little bubble shattered into a million pieces. I was as on edge now as I was looking for Channing and listening to him speak to the twins.

"Fuck," Penn muttered. Apparently he was thinking the same thing.

My heart in my throat, I stepped out into the corridor behind Asher and Zeke. I didn't miss the fact Penn moved into place on one side of me, Tully on the other. Landon and Channing walked behind me. My honour guard. Or bodyguards. Everywhere I went since the tour started, I went with the guys surrounding me like this. I couldn't decide if it was hot, scary or both.

There were worse things to be surrounded by than walls of muscle, especially when they knew how to take care of themselves. And me.

"We'll take the stairs," Zeke said.

No one questioned him. Not just because he was our unofficial leader, but because none of us wanted to get stuck in the elevator whether an attack took place or not.

Not even with six hot rock gods. Another time maybe, but not now.

Without a word, Tully took my suitcase and carried it in his other hand. I wanted to protest, but I would have dragged it down every step, bumping noisily as I went. Nothing about that said stealthy.

"When we get out onto the street, act naturally," Zeke said. "This was planned in advance, we know nothing about any plans that would stop us from doing what we're doing. We should meet Violet and the guys outside the front of the hotel. Jackson too. The vans shouldn't be long."

The calm in his voice was almost contagious. I wanted to believe nothing bad was going to happen. That we would get on our flight, fly to North

America and have a fucking good time putting on rock concerts. And then, go back to Australia and live our lives.

Maybe if I thought about it often enough, that would be what happened.

And maybe little pink, polka-dot pigs would fly.

6

ABBIE

"THERE YOU GUYS ARE," Violet said as we stepped out the front door of the hotel.

It was still early, not much past seven a.m. The traffic moving past was light. The amount of people on the street was lighter still.

When we checked out, there was someone different working on the desk. Judging by the smells that came from the kitchen, the chef got some work done after his liaison over the kitchen table.

"Violet," Penn drawled. "Did you scare all the paparazzi away?"

"Penn," she said in the same tone of voice. "I told them you were coming and they ran for the hills."

I laughed as they flipped each other off.

"Whatever has to happen to ensure they're not here," Jackson said, his expression completely dead-pan. "I have to admit I hadn't thought of that. We'll have to try it next time." A hint of humour crept into his eyes.

Penn swivelled his hand to point his middle finger up at Jackson instead. "I told you the paparazzi was scared of me."

"Actually, what you said is you're good at telling them to fuck off," Asher said helpfully.

Penn swivelled his finger towards him.

"Hey," Asher protested. "What did I do?"

"I don't know," Penn said, "but I'm sure you're about to do something. You usually are."

"Just because that's true doesn't mean I don't feel attacked," Asher said.

"Are you sure you wouldn't prefer a desk job?" Zeke asked Jackson.

"I'm more or less sure," Jackson said.

"Hey, whose side are you on?" Asher asked Zeke.

"Ours," Zeke said. He snaked an arm around Asher's neck and pulled him in for a kiss. Asher made a sound like he might refuse, but he kissed him back.

I couldn't help but watch. Ever since the first

time I saw them kiss, I'd enjoyed the view. They had the best friends to lovers love story, possibly ever.

"I'd tell you to get a room, but Zeke was the one who was all about hurrying us out of ours," Penn said.

Zeke broke off the kiss but kept his arm around Asher's shoulders. "If you don't want to see, then don't look." He seemed chill on the outside, but his eyes took in everything around us. Every person that went past, every car. He was a master of being vigilant without looking like it. If you didn't know him well enough, you'd easily be fooled.

At least to some extent, I was projecting my anxiety, but I knew he was on guard against everything.

I laced my fingers in Penn's. "Are you just wishing we had a room?" I asked teasingly.

He smiled down at me, then leaned to press his forehead lightly against mine. "Always, gorgeous. It's never not a good time for a nap." His body vibrated with laughter.

I slapped him lightly on the chest. "I didn't mean napping, and you know it."

"If Penn wants to nap, then it gives the rest of us the chance to fuck," Tully said. "So I say, let the man nap."

Without moving his head, Penn said, "The man will nap after a long, slow fuck." He lowered his mouth to mine for a long, slow kiss, his tongue sliding across my lips.

I closed my eyes and let out a soft moan. He was making me ruin my panties, one word and breath at a time.

He broke off and gripped my chin between his thumb and forefinger. He firmly turned my face until another set of lips found mine.

My eyes flickered open and I found myself looking at Tully. I kissed him deeply as I had Penn.

"Now who needs to get a room?" Asher teased.

"Who needs a room when you got the wall of the hotel right there?" Penn asked.

Holy shit, if I wasn't wet enough before, I was now. I broke off from Tully and looked over at Penn, who still held my chin.

"It's broad daylight," I squeaked. "And we could come under attack any minute now."

"You still want to," he stated. He slid a hand down my side and grabbed my ass.

Did I ever? I wanted him to press me back against the brick, lift up my skirt and impale me on his cock. I wanted him to fuck me until I screamed, and I didn't care who saw.

I swallowed hard.

"The van is here," Jackson said regretfully.

I didn't need to look at him to know he was turned on, I heard it in his voice. At least to some extent, he wanted to watch that happen, or wanted to do it himself. I was definitely going to have to find time to have that conversation with him. I cared about him too much to leave it for too much longer.

A quick glance in his direction confirmed my suspicion, but then we were all grabbing suitcases and pulling them forward to so they could be loaded onto the van. It was no tour bus, that was for sure. No blaze of glory. This was more a quiet retreat from Frankfurt.

Jackson and Zeke supervised the loading of the suitcases, while Penn, Asher and Tully herded me onto the bus, followed by Channing and Landon. Violet and her guys were right behind them, but they sat at the front of the van while the guys and I sat at the back. Penn manoeuvred me so I sat between him and Tully on the back seat.

"Finally, I feel like one of the cool kids," Tully said.

"When were you not one of the cool kids?" I asked him. He was one of the coolest guys I knew.

"I wasn't cool when I was a kid," he said. "I was a big nerd."

"What a shock," Penn said sarcastically.

"As if you weren't," Asher said to Penn. "I bet you were the biggest nerd of all of us."

Penn shrugged. "I never said I wasn't. I still sat on the back seat of the bus with my friends, because fuck authority."

"Penn, the rebel," I said.

He tangled his tattooed hand in the hair at the back of my neck and smiled. "You better believe it, gorgeous. Then and now." He kissed me, pressing me back until I was leaning against Tully.

Tully twisted little to the side and put his hands on my arms to hold me.

"The van has tinted windows, right?" I asked as Penn kissed my jaw and down to my neck.

"Yep," Penn said against my skin. "But anyone in the bus can see."

Good point.

I glanced around to see Violet chatting to Ryan, who sat beside her. He was looking at her like he might kiss her at any moment, if he dared.

Landon and Channing sat in front of us, talking in low voices. I caught a word here or there but not most of it. From what I could tell, they weren't discussing anything too intense.

Jackson sat across from them, his legs on the seat, his feet dangling off the side. If he turned his face a little, he could see everything we were doing.

Zeke and Asher sat in front of him, also talking to each other in low voices. Every so often, one or the other would look out the window, then they'd go back to talking. They were like a couple of soldiers making battle plans, or guards on watchful duty. Either way, the pretense of being chill was gone, unnecessary since no one outside could see us.

"See, no one is looking," Penn said. He kissed my neck and down to my chest before he tugged down the front of my shirt and peeled away one cup of my bra. He teased my nipple with the tip of his tongue.

I had a feeling I was being watched, and not just by Tully, who was still holding my arms. I looked over to see Jackson watching. I offered him a smile.

He swallowed hard in response, but didn't look away.

"You want to be with him, don't you?" Tully whispered in my ear.

I looked up towards the roof of the van. "Yes, but we're not ready yet." It wasn't just about having sex with him, that would be easy. It was about figuring where our boundaries were and where he factored into this crazy pack of ours. The guys in the band were all for it, but Jackson himself might not be. That didn't mean he couldn't watch though. If he objected, he could either look away or tell us to stop, and we would.

"All the more for us in the meantime," Penn said, his mouth full of my nipple. His hand wandered up my thigh. When his fingers grazed the front of my panties, they were covered from view by the fabric of my skirt. I was grateful for that. I wasn't ready for Violet and her guys to see my naked pussy, if they happened to look back this way. My breasts were one thing, that was another.

He tugged my panties aside and dipped his fingers into the wet well of my pussy.

I shivered with delicious anticipation.

"You like that?" he asked.

I murmured something incoherent.

"What do you say" he picked up his head to look me in the eye.

"Yes, sir," I said. "I like that very much."

"Of course you do," he said.

One of Tully's hands slipped down the front of my shirt and onto the breast which was still encased in a cup. He traced circles lightly around my nipple, then rolled it between his thumb and forefinger.

Penn hooked his fingers so they could massage my g-spot while he rubbed the heel of his hand over my clit.

"The drive isn't long, but I'm going to make you wait as long as I can."

Of course he would, because he was basically evil. Okay, that might be an exaggeration. He and Channing were the worst teases though. And I was here for every second of it.

"What if I don't want to wait?" I said breathlessly. I stuck out my chin like I really intended to rebel.

"You'll do as you're told or I'll turn you over and smack your ass until it's red," Penn growled.

I laughed low in the back of my throat. "You're going to threaten me with a good time?"

"It won't be a good time when you have to sit down for ten hours, but your ass is too sore," Penn said.

"Then I'd have to lie down," I pointed out. "That doesn't sound so bad."

"Don't tempt me, woman." He narrowed his eyes at me and worked me harder with his hand.

"If you keep doing that, I'm not going to be able to stop myself," I said.

"So you want me to stop?" He started to pull his hand out.

"No," I said quickly.

He quirked an eyebrow at me.

"No, sir," I said. "Please don't stop." Although, I had a handful of guys who would have helped if I asked them to, and we both knew it. No doubt he'd prefer to finish what he started as much as I wanted him to.

"Tully, do you think we should give her what she wants?" He looked over the top of me. "She might be too naughty to feel good."

"I think we should definitely give her what she wants," Tully said.

They must have exchanged a look I couldn't see, because Penn put his hand out and placed both of them on my hips. He rolled me over so I was face first across both guys, my face in Tully's lap.

"Hey." I grinned.

Tully tangled his fingers in my hair. "Hello there." His cock got hard under my cheek. I could feel the strain under the denim of his jeans, aroused, needy, wanting me.

Penn pushed my skirt up to my waist. "Good thing you're wearing a G string," he said. "Easier to get at bare skin."

He brought his hand down on my ass hard enough to make a loud slap. If everyone in the van didn't hear that, they would have heard my squeal.

I glanced over to see Violet look at me over her shoulder, but she smiled and went back to her conversation. I guessed she was used to our craziness by now.

Everyone else turned around to watch as Penn spanked me again. This time was harder, but made me groan in pleasure. The sharp sensation that coursed through me stoked the fire in my core and left me drenched.

He spanked me twice more, three times, each more painful and wonderful, then said, "Free Tully's cock and suck him."

"Yes, sir." With pleasure. If Tully was any harder, he'd break the zipper.

It took me a moment to catch my breath, and blink away tears from the stinging.

Penn hadn't held back and I loved that, but it was going to hurt as much as he promised. I loved every moment.

I undid the front of Tully's jeans until his erection popped out, then, my eyes on his face, fastened my lips around him and licked and sucked while he moaned.

"Penn has some good ideas," he ground out.

"Of course I fucking do." Penn slid his fingers into my from behind, two or three inside my pussy and his thumb inside my ass. "That's why you should listen to me more often."

Mercilessly, he fucked me with his hand, skilled fingers playing my saturated pussy like I was another instrument he'd mastered.

"Shit," I said around the substantial mouthful of Tully's cock. I teased his piercing with my teeth and lips, gripping and tugging gently while he groaned and fucked my mouth slowly.

"I want you both to come," Penn said, working me harder while he pinched my ass with his spare hand.

The pleasure, the pain, the wet smacking sounds of my mouth and my pussy drove me quickly to the edge and over, riding Penn's hand in almost fevered desperation.

I cried out, then clamped my lips down harder as Tully came, thrusting furiously before he stilled and squirted his salty cum deep in the back of my throat.

I was still lost deep in my orgasm when I swallowed down his release and let Penn milk my body for every drop of pleasure. He was a master at making my orgasms last for days.

"Good girl," he said when I finally came back down to earth with a lazy bump.

I turned my head to see Jackson still watching. His expression was heated, drinking in every moment.

One of these days...

7

CHANNING

"We made it," Landon said.

The plane bumped lightly as it landed in LAX. The world rushed past the window in a blur. Landon prefered to sit by the window and I never argued with him. Partly because I wanted him to be happy and partly because I got to look at him and the view at the same time. That was a win as far as I was concerned. The fact he didn't hate me was the biggest win of all. I would never not be grateful for him for accepting me, flaws and all. He was the sweetest, best guy I knew.

"It's a miracle right there," I said.

He twisted around and flashed me a grin that made my heart skip and my pulse race. I was the luckiest guy in the world, in so many ways. Most of them revolved around Landon, Abbie and the band. What was I saying? All of them revolved around those three things. I think I already established that I'd do anything to protect my world.

I smiled back and when he turned away, I let my gaze slide over to the seat beside us, where Abbie had just fastened her seatbelt. She'd spent most of the flight lying over Asher and Zeke, claiming her ass was too sore for her to sit for very long.

If she wasn't cheerful about it, I'd be mad at Penn. Not the spanking, that part was all in fun and fully consensual, but I worried he'd gone a bit too hard.

Still, she was smiling as she wriggled in her seat and winced. By the look on Asher's face, he found all of this hilarious. Penn, who sat the next row over, looked smug and pleased with himself. Of course he would, he was Penn. When was he not smug and pleased with himself?

Tully, like me, looked like he wanted to get some ice to ease her discomfort. Although, knowing him it wasn't just about discomfort. It would be about her experiencing the cold on her bare skin. He was all about heightening sensory awareness and being at one with the universe or something like that.

I don't know, it wasn't my thing, but I appreciated that it was his. He was a good guy. It kinda sucked he wasn't into other guys, but that was life. I wasn't surprised to learn Asher and Zeke were into each other. We knew it long before they did, Landon and I. We talked about it a few times and wondered how long it would take them to realise they had the hots for each other.

I got it. Sometimes it was hard to see what was right in front of your face.

The plane taxied down the runway and over to one of those tunnels we'd disembark from. This was where a lot of people like us would have insisted on getting off first. We preferred to wait a few minutes and let everyone else clear out ahead of us. It saved us tripping over them and vice versa. According to Jackson, it was good manners or some shit. Whatever, as long as we all got off the plane in one piece.

Landon's sweaty hand gripped mine as we took off our seat belts and stood. "Do you think we'll be okay?" he asked. "I'm half expecting to get shot the second I step off the plane."

"You're not gonna get shot," I told him. "There's no way I'm going to let anyone hurt you. You know I can and will do anything to stop them." I gave him a meaningful look.

He squeezed my fingers. "Not without me you're not," he said firmly. It was adorable when he got all bossy. We had long since established that I was the bossy one of the two of us. He was the sweet puppy who followed along, scared he'd get left behind if he didn't.

Yeah, I admit, that chafed from time to time. He knew I wasn't going to leave him, but sometimes he lets his insecurity get the better of him. One of these days, he'd understand and accept that he was stuck with me. In the meantime, I let him stick close if that was what he needed.

"Right, not without you," I agreed. As much as I liked to think he wasn't capable of killing anyone, he'd also do whatever he had to do to keep the rest of us safe.

Then, he'd discover that once you did it once, it was easier to do it again. Even Tully, who only killed for money once, had killed since. He claimed to hate it, but sometimes it was necessary.

"Keep your eyes open," I said.

"Not too open," Zeke said as he stepped out from in front of his seat, Asher right behind him. "Remember to play it cool. They don't know we know they're coming. If they notice us acting stranger than usual, they may try something rash. That won't end well."

"For them or us?" Abbie asked. To my surprise

she stepped over to me and took my other hand. Out of all the guys, I was the one she'd spent the least amount of time with. She was busy with the other guys, I was busy with Landon, and I needed to let my boyfriend get to know her first. I was ready to jump right in from the moment I met her, but he was more restrained than that. If Abbie and I got too close too quickly, he would have freaked out.

Sometimes, you have to play the long game in life and love.

"For them," Zeke said firmly. "The only thing that worries me about that is if we leave too much mess behind. Not to mention collateral damage."

"That would be bad," Asher said.

"Very bad," Zeke agreed. He waved us ahead of him and walked beside Asher as we made our way to the door.

Penn and Tully had moved first, making sure Abbie was right in the middle of us as usual.

She was a rose surrounded by six thorns. Seven if you counted Jackson, which I pretty much did already. That was another thing I knew long before they figured it out for themselves. The way he looked at her and acted all protective of her, he didn't act that way towards the rest of us.

At first, I thought it was because she was a

woman and had been through so much. Then I realised he fell for her the same time I did.

For different reasons, he held back too. For one thing, he wouldn't want to get accused of sexual harassment if Abbie didn't feel the same way he did. That kind of thing ruined careers faster than anything that ever happened to her. He also wouldn't have wanted to ruin the relationship he had with her and with us.

There was a lot at stake, but this was the way Wolf Venom did things. We jumped in hard and ran until we passed the finish line. And then we went on running. No one could ever accuse us of doing things by halves. We'd always been a driven group of assholes.

Somehow, Jackson was in front of us when we stepped off the plane and walked through the tunnel. We all ignored the flight attendants who stared at those of us who held hands. That now included Zeke and Asher. I was surprised the paparazzi hadn't picked up on that yet. They would, soon enough.

Fortunately, our fans were used to the relationship between Landon and I. They wouldn't bat an eye at Zeke and Asher.

I didn't know what they would think if they knew Abbie was with all of us, and frankly I didn't really give a shit. Our business was making music. They didn't really need to know what we did in private.

"We should be fine in here," Zeke said, keeping his tone conversational. "They won't want to try anything with all these people here. It wouldn't go unnoticed."

Penn snorted. "That's a fucking understatement. It would be headline news in about three point two seconds."

"That slowly?" Asher asked. "I would have thought at least two point two."

Penn rolled his eyes. "It takes time to record the words and upload them to cyberspace."

Asher nodded as if they were actually holding a serious conversation for once in their lives. "That makes sense," he agreed.

"You two are absolutely nuts," Landon told them.

"That's us," Asher said cheerfully. "Nuts with big nuts."

"So you admit I have big nuts?" Penn asked.

Jackson cleared his throat. "Maybe we can get our suitcases and get out of the airport sometime today? I don't know about you, but Blazing Violet is ready to put on a concert tomorrow night." He nodded to where Violet and the guys waited over to the side of the airport, watching us impatiently. "If you don't want to, I'm sure they could headline for you."

"Only if you want a riot on your hands," Penn said. "I'm pretty sure you don't, so let's go." He waved as if he wasn't the one holding us up a minute or two ago.

"Have I mentioned recently you deserve a medal for putting up with us?" Asher said to Jackson.

"I'll settle for a pay raise," Jackson said, holding back a smile.

"Poor Jax," Abbie said. She put a hand on his cheek, I think to pat it, but her fingers lingered there for a bit too long. Their eyes locked and I know I wasn't the only one holding my breath.

Just when I thought they might kiss, they stepped apart and we hurried towards customs and the baggage collection area.

We wouldn't have any trouble clearing customs, because we were who we were. They only ever glanced at our passports and made sure we weren't carrying drugs. If we were, Jackson and Levi would make the problem go away. As long as it was dealt with before the press got hold of the story. If they did, it would be more difficult, but not impossible.

The things you could get away with when you had a shit load of money.

"Everywhere I look, I feel like people are staring at us more than usual," Landon said nervously.

"Of course they're staring, we're Wolf Venom," I said lightly. "Don't get paranoid."

"Too late." His hand trembled in mine.

I stopped and turned to face him, almost pulling Abbie off her feet. I shot her an apologetic look, then turned back to him.

"You are Landon Flynn. Bass guitarist for the best motherfucking rock band in the world. Men and women all over the world have photos of you on their phones. They fantasise about you and groove to your music. You are a certified badass. You're the kid who came from nothing and is now in Los Angeles ready to play one of the biggest shows of your career. You're one of the most amazing people I've ever met, and none of us is going to let anything happen to you. I'm proud of you. I love you. Okay?"

I kissed his mouth and tasted salt and coffee. His stubble scraped against mine. I could have felt that all day long. And all night.

"Channing is right," Abbie said. "You are a badass. You both are." When I leaned back, she kissed Landon, then me. Neither was a quick peck either.

She took her time, kissing us deeply with lips and teeth and tongue.

Finally, she stepped back and said, without any hesitation, "I love you both."

"I love you," Landon told her.

It took me a moment to appreciate the fact the opportunity I'd waited so long for finally arrived. This wasn't exactly how I wanted to tell her, but I would take it anyway.

"I love you too, beautiful," I said softly. That felt good. Better than good. She was gradually teasing out my deepest, darkest secrets.

And my deepest, lightest ones as well.

8

ABBIE

"LANDON TOOK ALL OF THAT WELL," I said.

The hotel rooms were nothing fancy, just a couple of beds in one and a couple in the other. Each had their own bathroom, which made it easier for us all to cycle through the shower. The downside was that the showers were too small for more than one person at a time. Usually, we made it work, but that wasn't going to happen today. There was barely room for one person to stand up, much less two or three.

Maybe that spoke volumes about how spoilt we were. Hashtag first world problems.

"Yeah, he did." Channing lay next to me on one of the beds, my legs draped over his. With one hand, he was idly playing with my hair and tracing circles over the side of my face with his fingertips.

For once, I had him to myself while Landon was in the shower. Not that I minded spending time with both of them, but this was a rare treat.

"So did you," Channing added. He twirled a piece of my hand around his fingertip. "Most girls would have freaked out and run away."

"I'm not most girls," I said. Obviously, because he was right. Most people, when learning one of their boyfriends did the things he did, would have bolted for the hills. Me? I got aroused. "In fact, I should say thank you."

He unwound the hair, then wound it up again. "What for?" He looked at me intently with his pretty, hazel eyes.

"Wanting to make my life easier by getting rid of the people who made it harder," I said. "I've spent most of the last couple of years trying to put on my big girl panties and get past... Well, the past. But every time Vance did something, including die, the press came to me with new questions. Usually Poppy Newton was the one asking those questions. Calista was a horrible person, and apparently Pete was stalking me. Who knows whether he had something in mind or not?"

"Stalkers usually have something in mind," Channing pointed out. "It's not normal behaviour to follow someone around and take photos of them. Unless you're paparazzi."

"I'm not sure what they do is normal," I said wryly. "But it's certainly more normal than what he was doing. You know, we were really worried about you that day. We thought you were the one who was dead in that toilet."

"I'm not that easy to get rid of," he said, not boasting, just stating a fact. "It's sweet that you were worried about me though." He leaned in and kissed my nose.

"I could say the same to you," I said. "You were worried enough to do what you did for me. How many other girls can say a guy went to those lengths for them?"

"Baby, there's two hotel rooms full of people who would have gone to those lengths for you. In fact, the rest of the guys are probably kicking themselves for not doing it before I did." He shrugged the shoulder that wasn't pressed against the mattress.

"Possibly," I said. "I mean, from what Landon said, he would have gone along with you." That was a given.

"The rest of them would too," Channing said.

"Zeke and Asher would have taken part. Tully would have given advice, and Penn would have stood guard and told the rest of us what we were doing wrong. But in the end, someone had to watch over you while I was fixing things. If someone else, like the evil twins, got to you while we were busy doing that, we would never have forgiven ourselves."

"I see you've given it a lot of thought," I said. "And planning." I wasn't sure if I should find that disturbing or admirable. It was definitely hot.

"Growing up, I didn't believe in love at first sight," he said slowly. "But now it's happened to me twice. Once with Landon and again with you. Just like I don't want anything or anyone to hurt him, I don't want anyone to hurt you either. I went into protective mode."

"Have you killed anyone for him?" I asked half joking.

He hesitated.

My heart stopped. "You have?" I whispered.

"No," he said finally. "But I thought about it."

"His mother?" I guessed. It didn't take a genius to realise who he meant. What she did to him was worse than anything anyone did to me.

"Yeah," he agreed. "I didn't because I know he

wants to reconcile with her. He couldn't do that if she was dead."

"No," I agreed. "He couldn't. Do you think it's possible?"

Channing frowned. "I don't know. Olive Flynn has never been the most stable person in the world. She makes Penn look like an absolute sweetheart. But when she and Landon get along..." He sighed. "Those are some of his happiest times in his life. All he ever wanted was for her to get well and for them to take care of each other. As long as both of them are alive, he's not going to give up on that."

"What about your family?" I asked gently. "Landon said they were difficult too. Let me guess, you're a long lost Fiorelli cousin?"

Nothing would surprise me anymore. Hell, I wouldn't even be surprised if I learnt I was related to them. Or the Brantley family. Or the Bell family for that matter. As long as I wasn't really Zeke's sister. That would be all sorts of complicated.

Channing laughed softly. "As far as I know, I'm not related to any of them by blood. My parents were very conservative. They don't believe people should get tattoos or body piercings or be gay. Or bisexual. Or pansexual. Or polyamorous. In their world, boy meets girl, they get married, lose their virginity to each other on their wedding night and have as many babies as they can. They didn't appreciate it when I suggested they had a breeding kink." He grinned cheekily.

I laughed softly. "They sound a bit like my parents. They weren't quite so conservative, but they expected me to be married by now and giving them a grandchild or two."

"And here you are, with seven guys who all love you," he said. "What would they think of that?"

"I'm not sure," I admitted. "I don't think they'd want to know that you guys would kill for me. I think…" I chewed my lip for a moment. "I think if they met you guys and knew how well you took care of me and loved me, they would be happy for me. Once they got used to the idea." That might take them some time.

"And the grandchildren bit?" he asked. "Would they want seven?" He wiggled his brows slightly.

I groaned and tilted my head back. "I'm not sure I want seven. That would be a handful." I looked back at him. "Would you want one of your own?" That was the first question here. Well, the second after, 'did I want children at all?'

He pursed his lips. "Yeah, I think so. I kinda like the idea of a mini me running around. Also, it would piss my parents off. Not to mention the stir we would create with having seven children with seven different fathers." He grinned.

"Yeah." I laughed. "That would raise some eyebrows. Luckily, I don't mind raising eyebrows. As long as they don't get bullied for it."

"If any of them gets bullied, they'll have six siblings, seven fathers, and one amazing mother to back them up," he pointed out. "No one would dare. Not to mention, six of those fathers are members of Wolf Venom. We're the definition of badasses." He flexed his arm.

"Not to mention me," I said, giving a flex of my own. "All those last names would be confusing though. Unless they were all Hart."

"Baby, any kid of yours will be all heart," he said. He pressed his lips to mine gently. When he pulled back, he looked thoughtful.

"I know that look," I said. "You have a song forming in your brain, don't you?"

He grinned. "It's that obvious?"

"I've seen that expression in the mirror time or two," I agreed. "Inspiration comes whenever it wants to."

"True that. Let me see..." He scrunched up his brow. "Baby, you're all heart, you got in my head.

Baby, you're all heart, get in my bed." He chuckled. "Okay, needs a bit of work."

"Hey, it's a good start," I said. "And accurate, given we're already lying on one." I had a feeling he'd be balls deep inside me if Landon was here too.

As if he read my mind, he said, "Do you think it's weird that Landon and I like to be together when we're with you? I want you so badly, and if I was one of the other guys, I'd be fucking you so hard right now and making you wait to come."

"It's not weird at all," I said. "You have a special kind of relationship. Everyone has rules and boundaries, and you guys have yours. I feel like Landon would be… upset might be too strong a word, but if he walked in and we were fucking, I think that would be weird."

"But if you came out of the shower and we were fucking—" he looked at me questioningly.

"It wouldn't bother me because that's how our relationship works," I said. "I respect you and your respect for Landon. For the record, I want you too." Apart from the obvious exception of Jackson, Channing was the only one whose cock I hadn't had inside my pussy yet. In my mouth, yes, a few times. Quite a few.

"Can I ask you something?" I asked.

"Absolutely," he said. "At this point, I think you know all my secrets, so I have nothing left to hide."

"This is going to sound really weird," I said. "But when you… You know, killed and you know…"

"Cut their heads off?" he suggested.

"Yeah," I said. "What did you use? I keep wondering how you got knives past customs."

He gave me a knowing look. "You really want to know how I got knives past customs, or are you really wondering if I like playing with them?"

I licked my lips. "Both," I admitted. These guys had introduced me to a world of new things. The idea of Channing holding a knife to my throat with the same hand it used to kill turned me on way more than it should have.

He rolled me over into my back and straddled my hips. "I do like playing with them. Unfortunately, I didn't get knives past customs. I had to get rid of them before we went through the airport. But that doesn't mean I can't buy one for us to experiment with. Don't worry." He leaned down to nudge my cheek with his nose. "I know how to avoid cutting off someone's head."

"Well, that's a relief," I said. It was also a relief to know he did use a knife and not a guitar string. It might not have occurred to Landon yet, but I would bet anything Tully had thought of it. Hell, he probably knew exactly how to kill someone using a guitar string, then hide the evidence by stringing it on his own guitar.

And that wasn't even the most fucked up thought I'd had in the last few months.

"Let's call that a date," he said. "You, me, Landon and a blade."

"Lock it in," I agreed.

And there goes another pair of panties.

9

ABBIE

"ABBIE! ABBIE!" The crowds outside the hotel shouted my name, at least as often as they shouted the guys' names.

Not surprisingly, the press in LA were as hungry as they were anywhere else in the world. The tone was different though. Instead of being accusing or trying to dig up dirt, they seemed fascinated with the story of my twenty-six hour marriage and then the death of my ex-husband. Instead of being something tragic or terrible, they found it entertaining, like it was the latest Hollywood blockbuster.

I have to admit, that was the first time it occurred to me someone might actually turn that part of my life into a movie. I made a mental note to talk to Jackson about that. If anyone was going to do it, he'd know how to make sure I had a lot of say in it. Otherwise, I risked being portrayed in an ugly light and that wasn't something I was prepared to tolerate. Not anymore. I didn't expect to come out looking like an angel, but I also didn't want to be the bitch everyone ended up hating.

I waved and smiled while they took photos until Jackson herded us towards the tour bus that waited by the side of the road. Instead of saying *Wolf Venom* down the side, this one read *White Wolf Records*.

Asher nudged me with his elbow. "This is the bus the Rock Dragons tour on. When they're in the States anyway."

I nudged him back. He caught my elbow with his hand and tucked his arm through mine.

"It's adorable how you fanboy over another band," I told him. If I had to say who was bigger out of the two bands, I didn't think I could. They were both amazing and talented. Levi was lucky to have both of them on his label.

"You're never too old or successful to fanboy over someone else," Asher said. "Besides, my uncle Roman is their manager. I have to give them a little bit of loyalty."

"As long as it's not too much," Zeke said, hooking his arm through my other one. He grinned at the paparazzi as we walked past like that. "You know photos of you kissing Landon and Channing have gone viral, right?"

"Of course they did," I said. "And this will too. Maybe I should take this opportunity to make out with Penn and Tully just to round it all out."

"Don't forget Jackson," Asher said loudly. "If you're going to make out with them, then you should make out with him too."

When Jackson, who stood beside the door to the bus, turned to look at us, his face was pink. "Or we could get on the bus."

"Or both," Asher said unapologetically. He patted Jackson on the cheek on the way past. "You know you want to."

Jackson didn't meet my eyes as I stepped up onto the bus. We really, really needed to have that talk. If only to get Asher off his back if Jackson didn't feel the same way I did.

Who was I kidding? Asher would tease him anyway.

"Some people say seven is a lucky number," Asher said over his shoulder.

"And some people say *drum machine*," Zeke teased.

"Nah," Asher said, "a drum machine would take

up too much room on the seat. Although, they might vibrate just right."

"Are you trying to talk yourself into being kicked out of the band?" Penn shoved past Asher and flopped down into a seat.

"A drum machine still wouldn't be as hot as me." Asher sat in front of Penn and pulled me down onto his lap. He wrapped his arms around me and nuzzled his face into my hair.

"We could put a huge photo of you on the front of the drum machine," Penn said. "Then it would be just as good."

"He has a point, babe," Zeke said, grinning. "Then you can sleep in all day."

"As long as Abbie stays with me, then maybe you guys have a point," Asher said. "We can stay in bed all day and you guys can work."

"I'm having a hard time seeing a downside to that suggestion," I said. Except the fact I was still working at building up my bank account and didn't want to rely on the guys and their money for the rest of my life. They had enough, they wouldn't care, but I did. I had some pride left, and some desire to be independent.

"Exactly," Asher agreed. "Zeke could drop in after

work or whenever the band is in town." He sounded like he had it all thought out.

Zeke flopped down beside him. "You'd miss me too much. Both of you. You'd be bored after the first day or two. You thrive on challenge and applause."

"Just because it's true, doesn't mean you should come at me like that," Asher said. "I do like a good challenge. I don't need applause though, I could just download the sound of people clapping onto my phone and listen to that when I need it."

"That might be the saddest fucking thing I've ever heard," Penn said. "Also, it's bullshit. You like a live audience as much as the rest of us do." He crossed his arms over his chest and propped his feet on the seat.

Asher shrugged. "You're the ones who keep threatening me with a drum machine. I'm just trying to put a positive spin on it." Like always, he was clearly not worried about being replaced. It was the kind of running joke that would never die, even when its legs were getting tired.

"Besides, they don't need a keyboard player to sound good either. A decent quality synthesiser would do the trick." Asher made a face at Penn over his shoulder.

Penn responded by making a rude sound in the back of his throat.

"No one is going to replace you," I told him. I wiggled my hips into his groin and winced since my ass still hurt a little from Penn's spanking. If anyone was going to have to walk away when the tour was over, it was me. Not from the guys, they were stuck with me, but I wasn't a part of the band. We had yet to work out that complication. In the scheme of things, especially in the face of potential attack, it wasn't crazy important. We'd figure it out when the time came.

Asher winced too. "Tease. If you keep doing that, I'm going to come in my pants. Then you can explain to everyone why I have a big wet spot there." He twisted around in his seat and pointed at Penn before the keyboard player could say anything. "No, you can't tell them I wet myself."

Penn chuckled. "It would be accurate. Cum is wet."

"Yeah, but I didn't do it to myself," Asher said. "And anyway, they'd assume it's pee." He grimaced.

"You're a rock star, they'd assume it was exactly what it was," Zeke said. "But don't worry, if you need to come, Abbie and I have mouths you can do it in."

Asher groaned. "I knew there was a reason I loved both of you. I'm now the proud owner of a cock which is as hard as a rock." He pressed it against the side of my hip.

"I can feel it." I wriggled against him again, then slid down between him and Zeke. As fun as it was to tease Asher, the drive to the stadium wasn't long enough to ride him the way I liked to. When we arrived, we could find a place. And close the door, to make Jackson happy.

Violet and her guys piled on and the bus pulled away from the curb.

It would be nice to say we wove quickly and easily through Los Angeles traffic, but—it was LA traffic. No one in this city was going to pull over and let our bus pass, any more than they would in Sydney or anywhere else.

"Can you believe we're almost at the end of the tour already?" Asher asked. "It's gone by so quickly. It only seems like it started a couple of days ago."

"It only seems like a couple of days since I walked into the studio and met you guys," I said. And one more since I met Zeke and blew him off under the table without even knowing his name or who he was. If we ever had children, and they wanted to know how we met, we'd have to tell them it was at the label. They probably wouldn't believe the truth anyway.

Also, ewww, parent sex.

"I remember you were about to throw your shoe at Penn's face," Asher said.

"I'm not saying he wouldn't have deserved it," I said. "But that didn't cross my mind at the time. It was more fun to throw insults than shoes." Besides, I might not have gotten my shoe back from him. The way he was back then, he probably would have lobbed it out the window into the street, where it would have got run over by a garbage truck. Or, knowing my luck, an ice cream truck. Or one carrying chocolate and wine. Either way, my shoe would have been fucked and I didn't have the money to replace them.

"It still is," Penn said. "It takes more creativity to come up with an insult than it does to throw a shoe."

"Says the guy who can't throw for nuts," Asher said.

"Throwing inanimate objects is overrated," Penn said.

"As long as you don't say I'm overrated," Asher said.

"Now you mention it," Penn said slowly.

Asher flipped him off.

I turned to Zeke and said, "If I didn't know better, I'd think those two have the hots for each other. The sexual tension between them is off the charts."

"I've noticed that," Zeke agreed. To them he said, "I won't object if you to want two fuck."

"Me either," I said. "But can I watch?" I didn't think it would ever happen, but if it did, I was there for it. The idea of Penn on his knees, Asher's cock in his mouth, licking and sucking, was enough to make me drenched. The idea of Asher calling Penn sir did the same thing.

Hell yes, please. Just when I thought I'd run out of fantasies, there was always more to be had. I was here for that too.

"Absolutely," Asher agreed. "If Penn and I ever fuck, we want you both to be there. Don't we Penn?" He grinned over his shoulder.

"I definitely want everyone to be there," Penn agreed. "Because if that ever happens it's because I'm off my tree and probably need to go to hospital."

"That's a lot of words to say bring it on," Zeke teased.

"I'm starting to think you're as big a dickhead as your boyfriend," Penn said.

"That's not true," Zeke said. "You've known that for a long time."

"You said it, not me," Penn said.

I laughed and shook my head at all three of them. "And I'm starting to think you're all little boys still."

"That's more or less accurate too," Zeke said. "That's why you love us so much."

"Yes it is," I said. I couldn't deny the truth of that. Their love of life and tendency to grab each day by the balls and run with it, was part of their charm. It was addictive too. I'd done more living in the last couple of months than I had in my entire life. I worried less and less what people thought about me and enjoyed myself more and more.

"That and how adorable we are," Asher said.

He went to put an arm around me just as a loud bang sounded from the street outside the bus.

ABBIE

THE MANOEUVRE WENT FROM CUDDLING, to shoving me down so my face was on Zeke's lap.

I only had time for a grunt of surprise before Zeke was dragging me down onto the floor between the seats. The rest of the guys were right behind us, pressed around us. We were jolted as the bus slammed to a sudden stop.

"Is everyone all right?" Zeke asked urgently.

"Yeah," Penn said from a metre or two away.

"We're fine," Channing confirmed.

"It was a car backfiring," Tully said. He knelt beside a window and peered out.

"Cars still backfire?" Asher asked.

"Older cars," Tully said. "But given where we are, we can be forgiven for thinking it was something else, even if we weren't expecting trouble." He made a face. "Looks like everyone else made the same assumption."

"Stay down, just in case," Zeke told Asher and I. Keeping to a crouch, Zeke moved over to the window and looked out for himself. "Shit."

Because neither Asher or I were good at being told what to do, we both scooted over behind him and looked out.

Traffic had come to a complete standstill. The door of the car next to us was open as if the driver had climbed out and ran. Same thing happened with several in front of us. Annoying, but a sensible reaction if you think you hear a gunshot.

"I thought I told you to stay down," Zeke growled at us.

"You tell us a lot of things," Penn said, slipping back into his seat. "You expect us to remember all of it?"

"Just the shit that keeps you safe," Zeke said. He got to his feet and scanned the bus, inside and out. "It looks clear, but stay vigilant."

"This traffic isn't going anywhere anytime soon," Jackson said ruefully. "We're only about a mile from the stadium."

"It would be faster to walk," Tully said.

All eyes turned to Zeke. He thought for a moment, then nodded. "As long as we're careful, we should be okay to do that. Rather than sit here on this bus waiting for something to happen."

Jackson nodded. "The driver can make sure the bus gets where it's supposed to go. We'll need it to get back to the hotel later."

"Right." Zeke waved us towards the door. "Let's go. The bus will probably get to the stadium before us anyway."

"Maybe this was all an elaborate plot so the driver could have the bus to himself," Asher said. "Hey, Jackson, did you work with him, to make sure we get more exercise? This is the kind of thing you threaten us with." He narrowed his eyes, accusing but playful at the same time.

"I know I have exceptional organisational skills," Jackson said dryly, "but this is beyond even my abilities. Even if I could be bothered to do it, which I couldn't."

"Of course not," Asher said as if he didn't believe a word, but a smile tugged at the corners of his mouth.

Jackson's brow creased, uncreased, then he rolled his eyes at Asher. "If you don't hurry up, I might stay with the bus and make you stay here to keep me company."

"Now there's a good idea," Zeke said teasingly.

"Best idea I've heard all day," Penn said.

"Sometimes I really feel attacked," Asher said to me. He pouted.

I patted his arm. "Poor baby. Wasn't it you who said you're only nice to people you don't like?"

"I did, didn't I?" He looked more cheerful now. "Anyway, Jackson wouldn't want me to stay with him. He'd rather Abbie stayed." He stepped off the bus and looked at Jackson over his shoulder.

Jackson neither confirmed nor denied the suggestion.

I shrugged at him and followed Asher out, but my eyes lingered on his denim blue ones. Asher was definitely not wrong.

"Okay, everyone—" Zeke started to say, gesturing towards me to walk in the middle of everyone else.

"No," Penn said firmly. "You're going to stay in the middle." He pointed his finger, which was tattooed with an L, at Zeke's chest. "You and Abbie. If anyone is the target here, it's you. Fucked if they're getting past the rest of us."

Zeke raised his hands to either side. "Yes, sir."

Penn's eyebrows twitched. "Huh. That works in

all sorts of contexts. I like it. Right, everyone, get into place but look casual like Zeke keeps telling us to. Violet, you guys follow along at a bit of a distance. This doesn't involve any of you."

They looked only too happy to comply with that request, but no one from Blazing Violet called him sir. Penn looked a little disappointed at that, but nodded as Violet and the guys moved away.

"What we could use right now, is a pair of identical twin assholes," Penn said.

"They'd make good decoys," Tully agreed. "They're more likely to come under attack than Zeke and the rest of us, since they're closer to Reuben."

"Yeah," Asher said. "We could stick them out the front and hide behind them. Or better yet, stick great big targets on their backs."

"I like both of those ideas." Anything that kept us safe, I was all for it. Just because we'd agreed to work with the twins didn't mean we liked it, or them.

Personally, I would never forgive them for the things they did to us. Why should I? They were parasites. I wouldn't go as far as to say wanted them dead, but I wouldn't shed any tears either. Same with Reuben. Unfortunately, all three of them were probably like cockroaches—virtually impossible to kill, and often underfoot.

"Let's just not get lost." Zeke glanced at his phone and pointed. "We have to go that way."

We stepped off the street away from the stopped traffic. I glanced over at Jackson's expression as the bus door closed again. He was clearly as uneasy as I was.

Face down, heart in my throat, I followed the guys into the shade of a building.

"Should we be going straight there?" Asher asked. "Jackson might not have engineered this, but someone might have. If that's the case, they'll expect us to walk directly to the stadium."

"They know who we are," Tully said. "They'll expect us to take a different route there. If they planned this, then they planned for every possibility. The best thing we can do, is get the fuck out of the open and into the stadium."

"What Tully said," Zeke agreed. He looked over his shoulder to the bus too. He was obviously as happy with the situation as I was. He must have sensed my anxiety, because he laced his fingers in mine and said, "It'll be okay. We don't have far to go and there are people everywhere."

"You better be right," I said. "Unless you all have some power of invincibility you haven't told me about."

"Not invincibility, just caution." Zeke looked down at me as we walked. "You have it too, I've seen it."

"Yeah, I guess I do," I said. "Hyper vigilance is a symptom of PTSD, isn't it?"

"Something like that," Zeke agreed. A haunted look flashed through his eyes, reminding me I didn't know the half of what he'd been through in his life. We'd have plenty of time to find out if we didn't end up dead in the next couple of weeks. Or hours.

It wasn't just the warmth of the day that made me sweat. The whole situation had me on edge right from the moment I heard the bang. I felt vulnerable and I didn't like it.

"On the up side," Landon said more cheerfully than I'd seen him for the last day or so, "we're in Los Angeles, baby!" He swung his hand between him and Channing and grinned.

"Hell yeah we are, baby," Channing agreed. "I don't know about you guys, but I'm ready to rock the shit out of this town."

"Now that sounds like the best plan I've heard all day," Asher said. "Wolf Venom is here and were going to tear the world apart." He smiled and bowed at a couple of women who stopped to look at us as we walked past.

Specifically, to look at the guys as they walked past. They barely glanced at me.

Once, that would have pissed me off, but I was surrounded by seven hot guys whom I couldn't take my eyes off either. I couldn't expect anyone else to be any different. I could, however, be smug as fuck because all of them were mine. Let them stare, it couldn't do me any harm.

"Well, we were never going to be anonymous walking through Los Angeles," Tully remarked. He waved at a couple of young fans who squealed and took photos, eyes wide with excitement.

"It might be safer if we attract a crowd," Zeke said. "They're less likely to try something if we're surrounded."

"Less likely but not impossible?" I asked tentatively.

"No, not impossible," he agreed. "Idiotic though. They wouldn't get out of here with their butts intact if they did."

"No offence, but I'm more concerned with our butts than theirs," I said dryly.

"I'm more concerned with your butt and Asher's, because they're both so adorable," Zeke said. He slipped his hand out of mine and walked with his arm across my lower back, hand cupping my opposite ass cheek, thumb curled into the top of my skirt.

"Right back at you," I said lightly. I would have liked to enjoy this walk. It was a nice day. Like so many places we'd been to on this tour, I made a note to come back when we weren't so busy and under threat.

That begged the question… "Will there ever come a time when we don't have to look over our shoulders anymore?" It wasn't just this tour, I'd been watching over my shoulder since Vance admitted to marrying me to help his career along. It had become second nature and that wasn't okay.

His fingers squeezed my flesh. "Of course. We've already managed to get Reuben off our backs and we know we're not being followed by a stalker anymore." He gave a slight nod towards Channing.

"We just need to sort out this last problem and we're golden."

"You make it sound so easy," I said. We both knew it was going to be anything but easy. We could be dead by the end of the week. Or the end of the day. I didn't relish either of those ideas.

"It might not be," he agreed. "But we are us and we will deal with this. We're nothing if not awesome, but we're also skilled, vigilant and we've been warned, which chances are they have no idea about. Even if they do, we have a secret weapon."

"Penn's farts?" Asher suggested. "Those things are pretty deadly."

"He's referring to the way you bore people to death when you talk so much," Penn said over his shoulder. "Maybe we should let them abduct you. You could get rid of them for us."

"Between both of those things, maybe we should let them abduct both of you," Tully said. "They wouldn't stand a chance."

"I wonder if they would tie them to each other," I mused. That conjured up all sorts of fun, mental images.

Zeke grinned. "More likely handcuff them to each other."

"I'd pay to see that," Landon said.

"How much?" Asher asked. "Because if you're gonna pay, I could arrange that."

"No you fucking can't," Penn said. "There isn't enough money for me to put myself through that." After a moment he added, "But just out of curiosity, how much?"

Landon shrugged. "I dunno. A couple of hundred dollars?"

Penn scoffed. "Nowhere near enough. For a couple of hundred million, I'd consider it."

"Everyone has their price," Tully said. "Even Penn."

"Most of us would do a lot of things for a couple of hundred million dollars," I said. What wouldn't I do? Okay, I wouldn't kill for it. I wouldn't... No, that was about the only thing I could think of right now.

Tully stopped and waved for us to do the same. "Something's off," he said.

My heart skipped in my chest.

ABBIE

"STAY CLOSE," Zeke said urgently.

He gripped my arm to keep me tight beside him, his hip to mine.

"What is it?" I whispered.

"Hey, there you are," a voice said loudly.

I almost jumped out of my skin. One of the motherfucking evil twins, I think it was Hunter, appeared behind me and clapped a hand on my shoulder.

"Hey, Tully," Penn drawled. "You're right, something is off. Smells worse than my farts."

"You're hilarious," Hunter said sarcastically. He glanced over his shoulder. "Oi, Parker, they're over here."

"No shit," Parker said from right front of me. He

grinned when he saw my face snap around in surprise. "Lucky we're not here to attack you," he said as if he was hilariously funny. "None of you saw us coming."

"I think I speak for all of us," Asher started, "when I say none of us wants to see you coming."

I snorted a laugh. "Fuck no."

Penn offered Asher a high five. "Nice burn, dude."

Asher slapped his palm against Penn's and grinned. "I thought so, thanks."

Hunter draped an arm over Parker's shoulders. "Looks like we found the circus, bro."

"Yeah," I agreed. "We were waiting for the clowns, but you just got here."

The guys except for the twins looked impressed.

"Sweetheart, that was awesome," Zeke said. He leaned in for a quick kiss.

"It wasn't bad," Penn said. "I also would have settled for monkeys, performing bears, or freakshow acts."

"You guys should give up music and become stand-up comedians," Parker said, not looking the least bit offended. Unfortunately.

"You guys should give up breathing," Penn said scathingly. "Any number of us would be happy to help you with that."

Hunter clicked his tongue. "Have you already forgotten we have a deal? Because, if you have, we have a deal. You don't get to kill us and we don't get to kill you, or mess with you. Believe it or not, we're here to help. It took us a while to get through customs and find you guys, but here we are. Just a word of advice, you might want to be less predictable. If we found you, then they can."

"And if you hang around with us, they can find you too," Channing pointed out.

The twins exchanged a glance.

"He has a good point," Hunter said to Parker.

Parker shrugged. "Yeah, but a deal is a deal. We wouldn't want anyone to say we go back on our deals, would we?"

"Good to see you've narrowed in on the important things in life," Zeke said.

I couldn't tell if he was being sarcastic or not.

"We're good at doing that," Parker said lightly. "Hey, Abbie, ready for a real man yet?" He looked around Zeke and smiled at her.

"Fuck off," I told him.

I was tempted to tell him I didn't go for clowns, but no doubt they'd turn it into some kind of dig against the other guys.

"I think that's a not yet," Hunter said to Parker. "Give her time, she'll come around."

I grimaced at them. "Only when hell freezes over, asshole."

"The way climate change is going, that's a distinct possibility," Hunter said with a nod. "Until then, we'll wait patiently."

"I'm pretty sure there's a name for guys who come onto a girl when they have a girlfriend," I said.

"There's several of them," Zeke said. "And none of them are nice." He waved for us to get back into the loose formation we were walking in. "Let's keep going."

"I thought I was the general today," Penn said.

Zeke gave him a smirk. "Let's not have an argument over who's in charge. And don't get used to me calling you sir, either."

"Sounds like trouble in paradise," Hunter said, looking amused.

"Why do you care?" Zeke said. "It's not like you're going to replace either of us in the band. Reuben would never allow it." For some reason, he looked cheerful about that. Maybe it was knowing Reuben kept them on a short leash instead of him.

"Do we need a reason to care?" Hunter asked. He turned to Parker and said "I don't think so, do you?"

"As amusing as it is to stand here wasting time," Zeke said, his tone terse, "I'd rather get to the stadium. "Some of us have work to do." He gave the twins a meaningful look.

"Have you failed university yet?" I asked. "You're never there."

"The bitch has teeth," Hunter said. "I like that." He bared his at me.

I flipped him off.

"For the record," Hunter continued, "we're still on holidays. They end just after the tour is over. Isn't that convenient?"

"Almost too convenient," I agreed. I didn't know why they bothered going to school anyway. They had jobs working for Reuben that presumably paid well. They got to travel the world, meet interesting people and kidnap them. What more could anyone want?

"If I didn't know better, I'd think the tour was planned to coincide with the holidays," Hunter mused.

"Not fucking likely," Penn growled. "It wasn't planned for your convenience. It was planned so we could make a shit load of money."

"I thought you already had a shit load of money,"

Parker said. When Zeke and I started walking, he walked beside me, on the other side.

"A shit load more money," Penn said. "Enough money that we don't have to deal with dickheads like you."

"I hate to break it to you, but there's no amount of money in the world that can keep you from having to deal with people you don't want to deal with," Parker said with no hint of apology.

"Are you speaking from experience?" Tully asked. "You have plenty of money but you still have to deal with your brother Reuben?"

"Not to mention Zeke," Parker agreed. "He used to be fun, when we were kids. Now, he's all about work and telling us to go away. Not very brotherly, is it?"

"Kidnapping my girlfriend twice isn't very brotherly either," Zeke snarled. "Not to mention—" He stopped and took a deep breath. "You know what, it doesn't matter. You know what you did and why I'm pissed off at you pair of degenerate little pricks."

"Because they're degenerate little pricks?" Asher asked.

"Exactly," Zeke nodded in his direction. He pulled his phone out of his pocket and checked the screen. "It's just up ahead around the— Yeah, right there."

Like the average stadium anywhere in the world, this one was hard to miss. It looked like a cross between a low-lying spaceship and a... No, low-lying spaceship was basically it. Just past the stadium, water twinkled in the sunlight.

"You know what I wish?" Landon said wistfully.

"What do you wish, baby?" Channing said.

"I wish you could have that rematch with Penn here and kick his ass," Landon said. He gave Penn a sly look.

Channing sighed. "Me too, baby. Me too."

"In your dreams," Penn said scathingly. "I'd hand your ass to you like I did in Munich."

"Maybe," Channing said. "Maybe not."

"Do you think you could run faster than us?" Parker asked Penn.

Penn didn't break his stride as he looked Parker up and down. "I wouldn't bother. I'd wait until you started running, then walk off in the opposite direction. By the time you figured it out, you'd be a long way from me and I'd be happy."

"Sounds like he thinks he can't beat us," Hunter remarked.

"I can beat you all right," Penn said. "I'd rather use a baseball bat. Or a cricket bat. Or both, one in each hand."

"Has anyone told you you're very hostile?" Parker said lightly. "It can't be good for your blood pressure."

I hooked my fingers around Penn's arm before he rounded on them and actually started swinging. "They're just trying to get a reaction from you."

"It's working," Penn growled. He put a hand over mine and squeezed, probably firmer than he intended.

"When this is over, if you want to spank them, I'm here for it," I told him.

"Now you're talking," he said, his dark expression lifting slightly. "Not spanking them wasn't part of the deal."

"Don't bother," Zeke said. "They'd enjoy themselves too much."

"He's right, you know," Parker said. "We're into all sorts of interesting things, including that. When we were younger, we used to spank each other just to—"

Penn groaned. "Way too much information, dude. We don't want to hear about your kinky shit."

I kind of did. I mean, the mental image of the twins spanking each other was hot in all kinds of the wrong ways. I had to stop thinking about this before my mind went to cocks and mouths.

Oops, too late. Well, my panties were ruined already.

"Shame," Parker said. "I was hoping to hear about all of your kinky shit. I bet Abbie is really wild in bed." He gave me a speculative look.

I smiled back at him. "I absolutely am," I said unashamedly. "Wild like you have no idea. Wild like you're never going to find out."

Parker grinned. "Don't worry, my imagination is pretty healthy and you feature in a lot of my fantasies."

Zeke and Penn growled in unison. Zeke took a step towards his brother.

I grabbed him before he could go too far. "Don't bother. I don't care if he's thinking about me when he's jacking off. That's between him, his hand and his brain."

Parker gave Zeke a smug look.

"Does anyone know if there's a way to climb the top of the stadium?" Asher asked. "You know like, to abseil off it?"

"I don't think so," Zeke said. "Why, babe? You feel like climbing?"

"No, just thinking about where we could throw the twins where they wouldn't bounce," Asher said.

"Okay, fair enough," Zeke nodded. "I don't think

we can do it there, unfortunately. Also, they probably would bounce once or twice. I'm all for finding out at some point."

"You first, bro," Hunter said. "If you survive the experience, we'll consider doing it."

"Hard pass," Parker said. "I like my feet either on the ground or on the bed."

"I'm starting to think you two have sex on the brain even more than I do," Landon told him.

"That's saying something," Channing chimed in.

Parker shrugged. "We're nineteen, we're supposed to have sex on the brain. And on the bed. And on the beach. And on the kitchen bench. And—"

"Yeah, we get the idea," Penn said. "Maybe you can shut the fuck up."

"We'll think about it," Hunter said. "In the meantime, Zeke—"

"I've seen them," Zeke said. "They've been following us almost since the bus. Don't look around," he said to me just before I did.

"Who is it?" I wasn't over my unease, but it was a hundred times worse now.

"I dunno, maybe just fans." Zeke didn't look like he believed that himself. "Let's walk a little faster."

We approached the entrance to the stadium, and security waved us in.

"My boss knew you were coming," one of them said. He was about seven feet tall with dark skin covered almost entirely in tattoos. His ears were full of piercings, including an industrial bar across the top of one. He was the kind of guy you might be intimidated by until he smiled. Then, I got the impression he was a gentle giant.

"Thanks, bro." Asher offered him a high five. He winced at what must have been a hard slap by the guard.

"Wait till I tell my kids I met Wolf Venom," the guard said. "Go on in."

Asher shook his hand and we hurried inside.

12

CHANNING

"WE SHOULD BE FINE IN HERE." Zeke tried to look as calm and chill as ever, but I knew him better than to think he was actually relaxed. Once in a while, his eyes flicked towards the door.

"There's about a billion people inside the stadium," Landon pointed out. "They couldn't do anything without witnesses. Lots of them."

I knew he wasn't that naïve. If anything happened to us, it wouldn't go unnoticed for long, but that didn't mean it couldn't happen. Just because the security guard outside the door looked nice, didn't mean he wasn't on the Fiorelli payroll. Cleaners could pop up in toilets or someone could poison the sandwiches in the green room.

In spite of that, I said, "You're right, baby. Let's focus on the sound check."

"I thought this place would be more impressive," Hunter said, looking around the backstage area. "I suppose the stage is."

"You're not gonna get to find out," Zeke said. He grabbed Hunter's arm and pulled him aside. Whatever he said in his brother's ear, Hunter wasn't happy about it.

He sighed loudly and said, "If I have to. Come on, Park—"

"Just you," Zeke told him. "Parker can stay here with us. It's not healthy for you to spend all of your time with each other."

Both twins looked like they wanted to strenuously object, but Hunter nodded.

"Fine, I won't be long. Make sure security knows to let me back in." He strode out of the green room like he owned the place.

"I have a better idea," Penn said. "How about we tell security he can't come back in?"

I didn't always agree with Penn, but in this case I did. I'd spent enough time working with those shitheads, or trying to make them think I was working with them. They were useful up to a point. Most people wouldn't know how to get rid of human remains. The fact only they knew what they'd done with them and could put that over my head at any time made me nervous. If I hadn't agreed not to kill them, I would seriously consider it. What the fuck use were they anyway? I would have figured out something without their help if I had to.

"Did someone mention sound check?" Tully said cheerfully. "That sounds good to me."

"I'll go and see if they're ready for you," Jackson said. He glanced at Abbie, his gaze lingering a little too long, before he turned and hurried toward the stage.

"Did you finish the song you were writing?" Abbie asked as we slowly walked together towards the stage.

I looked over at her. I didn't know who I wanted to gobble up first, her or Landon. They both set my blood on fire like nobody else.

I smiled. "Not yet. I can't find a word to rhyme with threesome."

She glanced back at me like she wasn't sure if I was joking or not. "That is a difficult word to rhyme with. I'm guessing wholesome isn't the angle you're going for."

"I'm going for a bunch of angles, but not that one," I agreed. Angles, positions, I had a few of them in mind. All of them involved her and Landon. The other guys could watch and learn.

"I remember when touring used to be stressful," Landon said.

"You don't find this stressful?" I asked him.

He looked over at me and blinked. "Yes. No. I mean, I'm remember when the touring part was stressful. Now it's all the other shit. Although, there's still a threat of bees and tornadoes." He grinned at me.

I groaned softly and rolled my eyes. "It could still happen." And I was still freaked out by bees. That whole conversation felt like it took place months ago. I let my insecurity get the better of me, scared Landon would leave me for Abbie.

Yeah, okay, there was still a voice in the back of my head that had the same concern. He was sweet, and in some ways a lot more innocent than me. When we met, he was a lot more innocent. Some-times, I blamed myself for stealing that from him. Then I remembered, the world would have done it anyway and I needed him by my side. He was the spoonful of sweetener in a bitter coffee.

"You don't like bees?" Abbie asked.

"I like what they do for the planet," I said. "But I'll stay out of their hive if they stay out of mine."

"I have the same philosophy about sharks," she said.

"I could be wrong, but I don't think sharks have hives," Landon said jokingly.

We both made a face at him and laughed.

"Honestly, a hive of sharks sounds terrifying," she said. "How would you get the honey?"

I stopped and grabbed her arm in one hand and Landon's in the other.

"Like this." I lowered my mouth to hers and kissed her long and deep before doing the same to Landon.

"Nothing could be sweeter," I said softly.

"You're going to make us jealous," Asher remarked.

All of the guys stopped to wait and watch.

"Do you want me to kiss you?" I asked him.

"I would, but then Zeke would be jealous," he said easily.

"Yes, I would," Zeke said, but his tone suggested otherwise.

I didn't think a relationship beyond friendship was in the cards for Asher and I, but if it was, I doubted it would bother Zeke too much, as long as we communicated. For that matter, I didn't think Landon would mind, if he got to take part as always.

Ever since we met, he'd been all about making me happy, and doing whatever it took to for us stay together. Sometimes, that was his insecurity talking, his fear that I would leave, but I got it. It took time for him to understand I was never, ever going to walk away from him, but every moment of that was worth it.

Landon was, and always would be, my person.

"I don't object if you guys spend more time together," Penn said. "You can even take Tully with you if you like."

Because I knew him too well by now, I said, "Here's where you say we should leave Abbie behind, but it's not gonna happen, dude."

Penn shrugged as though he hadn't just been called out. "A guy can hope." He continued the walk down the corridor as a woman who worked for the stadium beckoned us forward.

She was lucky she only saw us standing there. If we were there much longer, she would have seen someone fucking someone up against the wall.

"A guy can be an arrogant pain in the ass too," I said.

"Yes, you can," Penn said over his shoulder.

Shame he had his back to me, he didn't see me

stick my finger up at him. No doubt he felt it. The guy could be such an asshole sometimes.

I have to admit, I was conflicted over the way he treated Abbie when they first met. On one hand, I wanted to do everything I could to protect her. On the other hand, he was my brother. I wouldn't have killed him, but I thought about scaring him a little bit. In the end, I decided against it because I saw the way he felt about her, and knew he'd come around eventually. Waiting for that to happen almost killed *me*, but he got there in the end.

Lucky for him.

"Hey, that's not nice," Parker said to us both. "You guys can be so mean to each other."

"Thanks," Asher said, "but we don't need your permission."

I snorted a laugh, then snorted again at the expression on Parker's face.

"That wasn't what I was saying." He frowned.

"No one gives a fuck what you're saying." I wished he would fuck the fucking fuck off and never come back.

That night in Frankfurt, I had seriously considered killing them both. Part of me regretted telling Zeke I was meeting them. In the end, I had no choice, he'd figured out I was up to something.

Either way, he would have followed me. Same with Landon, Abbie and Jackson too.

Everything would have been a thousand times messier than it already was. Messy enough that it was worth putting up with the twins to avoid it. For now. The sooner they were out of our hair, the better.

"Hunter does," Parker said.

"Are you sure about that?" Abbie asked. "I mean, he might put up with you because you're twins. Or out of habit. Or because Reuben told him to."

"No wonder you hang out with these guys," Parker told her. "You're as mean as they are." He didn't look particularly offended.

"What does that say about you, then?" she asked him. "You've followed us around since before the tour began. What is it they say? Birds of a feather —"

"Fuck together," he finished for her and grinned.

"*Flock* together," she said firmly.

"You really should finish that degree, bro," I told him.

"Bro," Parker said to me, looking down his nose. "I'm not studying English literature."

"No, you're learning advanced stalking," I said. "This is your practical component."

Parker laughed. "You're hilarious."

"I'm not that far wrong," I said.

Abbie gave me a funny look.

"He goes to Brutham Academy," I told her. "Most of the students there have families like ours. They call it Brutal Academy. It's the only university in Australia where the mortality rate is higher than the dropout rate."

Her eyes widened. "That's where Asher's brother Dane works?" she asked.

"The very same," Asher agreed. "I almost went there but then I realised something. I didn't want to." He smiled with his mouth closed, all sarcasm.

"Same here," Zeke said with a rueful look and a nod. "Dad and Reuben both tried to get me to go, but I declined politely."

I took that to mean he told them to fuck off. Considering the suggestion, that was an appropriate response as far as I was concerned.

"You don't know what you're missing," Parker said.

"The students really die?" Abbie asked me.

"Yes, they do," Parker said before I could reply. "Every year before the end of the second semester, the Academy likes to test students' skills. Things have been known to get ugly."

"How is that allowed?" Abbie asked.

"When you have money and connections, everything is allowed," I said. "Bribe the right people and they'll turn a blind eye to anything. Even exam month at Brutham Academy."

"So there's a chance you and Hunter might die before you graduate?" Abbie asked. Both of her perfectly shaped eyebrows rose and I swear her blue eyes became a brighter shade.

"It's a very slim possibility, but you don't need to look so hopeful," Parker said. Now he looked offended.

"I speak for all of us when I say we're definitely hopeful," Penn said. He glanced back and gave us a meaningful look before stepping out to the stage where a bunch of people stood, watching and waiting.

His silent condemnation had a point. We should probably not talk about the Academy in front of other people. For some reason, regular people didn't understand. Yeah, okay, neither did I. Sure, families wanted their kids to be the best of the best, but to die because they weren't? That seemed tiny bit extreme to me.

As everyone filed onto the stage, I managed to grab Zeke's attention.

"Where did you send Hunter?" I asked him quickly.

He glanced at me over his shoulder. "To go and look for any sign of trouble. If anyone can find it, it's him."

"Right," I said softly. He wasn't wrong about that. The twins seemed to be attracted to trouble like they wanted to fuck it. Or they were the cause of it. Either way, trouble was both of their middle names. That and Prick from Hell.

I trotted up the steps and tried to focus on the job ahead: sounding fucking awesome for tonight's audience.

13

ABBIE

"G'DAY," Zeke said into the microphone. "How's it going today? Thanks for coming out." It was only the sound check, but his accent was stronger than usual.

For some reason, Americans seemed to like Australians, so he might have done it consciously for that reason. Either way, it was kinda cute, although I'd never heard him say *g'day* before.

The handful of stadium staff who gathered around to watch clapped, and a couple cheered. It must be fun to work in a place where you got to live these moments once in a while. Most of them would probably come back tonight for the concert, but they got this for themselves.

"We're from a little island down south a ways.

You might know it." Zeke grinned at Penn as the keyboardist rolled his eyes at him.

"He's laying it on a bit thick," Jackson said. He stood beside me, leaning against the wall.

"They seem to be eating it up," I said. Here we go again, tripping over innuendos.

Jackson cleared his throat. "Yeah. Zeke always has a way of knowing what the crowd likes. It's one of the things that makes him such a good lead singer."

"It is," I agreed. "Maybe I should speak with a broader accent tonight?" I looked up at him questioningly.

He looked down at me and smiled. "Just be yourself. That's plenty."

My heart skipped a beat like it was jumping a rope. It really was impossible not to adore him.

"You think so?" I asked.

His gaze lingered on mine. That look conveyed so much, without him saying a word.

"Yes, I think so," he said, his voice low but firm. "You live life unapologetically. There's no reason to change that now."

I was surprised for a moment but then I nodded. "I do, don't I?" Okay, there were moments there when I wanted to hide from the world, but we all had those. Right?

"More than anyone else I have ever met," he said. "With the possible exception of Asher. I don't think he's held back a day in his life."

"Only when it came to his feelings for Zeke," I agreed. "But that was more about him waiting patiently and coming to a realisation, than holding back. Did you know there was something between them before they did?"

Jackson chuckled. "Only from the first time I met them. I was starting to think I was wrong, but I guess I wasn't. Like I said to you once before, you helped them to connect. If not for you, they'd probably still be nothing more than best mates."

I waved a hand dismissively. "They would have figured it out."

The clash of Asher's drums echoed through the stadium. Landon was half a beat behind, but he quickly caught up. The rest of the instruments followed.

It wasn't like Landon to be off like that, but we were all under a lot of pressure. The audience wouldn't have noticed anyway, especially with them cheering and screaming. Knowing Landon, he'd beat himself up over it, but we'd help him through it. No one ever said musicians weren't temperamental as fuck. We all were, but we got each other. Most of the time.

"They might," Jackson agreed. "Sometimes it takes time to see what's in front of you." He was looking at me again.

I looked at him and swallowed. "Yeah, it does."

He leaned down to brush his lips lightly over mine. It was barely more than a graze, but it set my heart racing and made my knees weak. He tasted of coffee and something I couldn't put my finger on. Maybe with a longer kiss, I could work it out.

He straightened and leaned back against the wall as though nothing happened.

I waited, catching my breath and giving him time to gather his thoughts.

After a minute or two, he said, "I'm sorry should I have—"

"Done that sooner?" I asked, knowing that wasn't what he was implying. "Probably."

"It could complicate a lot of things," he said.

"Then we'll deal with it like we deal with everything else," I said firmly.

"With sex and alcohol?" he teased. The lines around his eye crinkled.

I laughed. "I see nothing wrong with that." I leaned against him and he placed a hand under the back of my neck, under my hair. Nothing about this felt strange at all. I'd stood like this with all the other guys dozens of times in the last couple of months. To do it now, with Jackson, felt natural and right.

"Don't tell me, you're going to have to tell Levi." I was only half-joking.

"At some point," he admitted. "Let's see where this goes first. The guys might..."

"They already know," I said. "And they're fine with it. I mean, I told them how I felt about you. I wasn't assuming anything."

"I guessed," he said quickly. "You would have assumed right. I cared about you the moment we met. Actually, before that. Would you believe I've been to a couple of your concerts with some friends?"

For some reason, I found myself blushing. "You did? Wait, did you say a couple? As in more than one?"

He grinned. "Does it surprise you so much? You're talented and gorgeous. You had fans before all the things that happened at Onyx Riot. I happened to be one of them. When Levi mentioned wanting to sign you, I might have encouraged him."

"Right," I said slowly. "So everything that

happened after that is all your fault." I poked him playfully in the chest with a bright pink fingernail.

"Yes," he said ironically. "None of that had anything to do with those outside influences. It was all me."

"You would never do any of those things," I said. "You're a good guy."

He shot me a lopsided smile. "Not a very professional one right now."

"The heart wants what the heart wants," I said.

"Yes, it certainly does," he agreed. "Seeing you in concert, I never would have thought— I mean, of course not. That would be presumptuous."

"Sometimes fantasies come true." I had fantasised about this very moment a few times myself. Yes, even with six other guys keeping me busy, there was time for fantasies. What was the fun in life if you couldn't daydream once in a while?

"I'll be the first to admit I didn't think it would turn out like this," he said. "As soon as Zeke took an interest in you, I figured that was that. Being your manager, anyway, it was safer to step back and try not to think too hard about you. But then, you have a way of getting under people's skin and into their hearts. I can't say I resisted too strongly."

He paused for a moment before he continued.

"Then with everything else going on, I wondered why I was resisting at all. Life is usually short. Lately, it seems like… Like if we don't grab hold now, we may lose our chance. I didn't want that to happen. For the record, I wouldn't do what Channing did, but there's a lot I would do for you. For the guys too. We might be the weirdest family, but we're still a family. One I happen to be attached to. No matter what might happen. I'll take this over a desk job any day."

"Is Levi going to be pissed?" I asked. "Does he really have a girlfriend?"

"Probably not, and yes," Jackson said. "He'll be pissed if I screw you over, and her name is Charlotte. She is a lovely woman but I don't think she is going to end up with seven partners."

"Not everyone is the sharing type," I said. "So no screwing me over, hmmm? What about screwing me?"

His face turned slightly pink. "I don't think we should rush, but…"

That was all the response I needed. If he was one of the other guys, I might have dragged him away to some quiet place in the stadium and fucked his brains out. But he wasn't one of the other guys.

"How are you single?" I asked without thinking.

"Am I single?" he asked with one eyebrow raised. He must have realised he put me on the spot, because he said, "That's a conversation for later." He stroked his thumb over the back of my neck. "I was married once and it didn't work out. Ever since then I've focused on work. Until you came along and turned everything upside down and inside out."

"Sorry, not sorry," I said lightly. He seemed sad, remembering her. Whoever she was, she must have been amazing to have caught his attention, even if it wasn't meant to be. He was an extraordinary guy.

As for turning his life upside down... I seemed to have a knack for that.

"You certainly have nothing to be sorry for," he said. "We could all use a shakeup. Wouldn't want the boys to get stale, would we?"

I snorted. I doubted that would happen. "No way," I agreed.

"It's time for you to go out there and sing with Zeke," he said with a touch of reluctance.

I felt that a little bit myself. It wasn't how I pictured having this conversation, but I felt better for having had it. It was like the last piece of the puzzle fell into place. I might have also liked the fact we were now an even eight.

"Yes, boss," I said with a cheeky grin.

He gave me a heated look. "Be careful, I might get used to hearing you call me that."

I didn't need to look down to know I would see a tent in front of his pants. I totally caught the same vibe.

"I don't have a problem with that." I brushed my lips over his. In heels, we were almost the same height. Close enough for me to look into his pretty eyes.

"Me either." He patted my ass and gave me a gentle shove towards the stage.

"All right then, boss," I said grinning over my shoulder. I barely heard him groan before I trotted up the steps and onto the stage.

Zeke caught my expression and gave me an amused smile.

"Welcome back to the stage," he said, his accent still broad.

"Thanks, mate," I said as I grabbed myself a microphone. "It's fair dinkum, bloody awesome to be here, ay?"

Zeke burst out laughing. "Yeah, mate. It's the bloody roo's pyjamas."

"Wouldn't that be a pouch?" I asked.

Zeke shrugged. "Crikey, you might be right."

I shook my head at him.

Tully grinned over the top of his hot pink guitar.

In the corner of my eye, I caught Penn cringing. Apparently not everyone appreciated our attempts to embrace our Aussie culture.

You can't please everyone.

Zeke and I started to sing "Take Me down Lower", while around a hundred stadium staff danced in front of the stage

Outside the front of the stadium, fans were probably doing the same thing. It was the perfect day for it, if it wasn't for everything else that was going on. Right now, that seemed like a million kilometres away.

I spied Jackson as he walked around from backstage to the front of it. He stayed back from the crowd until a man in a stadium uniform came over to speak to him. Whatever it was the man said, Jackson didn't look too worried. He nodded and gestured before following the man out of sight.

Presumably the bus finally turned up. Thank fuck for that. I didn't relish the idea of walking all the way back to the hotel. Not that we would, since taxis and ride shares were a thing. Still, most of those didn't fit eight of us and five of Blazing Violet. And a stray twin or two.

Parker sat in a seat off to the side, elevated for a

good view of the stage. There was no sign of Hunter. What had Zeke sent him to do? I was sure I would find out soon enough. For all I knew, he sent his brother to get some chocolate. If he was going to hang around, then he might as well be useful. And what could be more useful than getting food?

We finished the song and launched into "Bump in the Night". I was pretty well acquainted with both songs before the tour, but I'd sung them so many times now I knew them as well as I knew any of my own music. Singing with Zeke was a different experience from singing by myself though. We complimented each other so well on and off stage. Like Tully would say, the universe made us all for each other and now we'd found each other.

I just hoped we weren't about to lose each other.

14

ABBIE

"Where is he?" I glanced around the room and at my phone for the millionth time. "I haven't seen Jackson since sound check." I thought he'd be waiting for us backstage, but he wasn't. We'd decided to wait in the green room for him but he hadn't shown up yet. That was out of character for him. He wasn't our shadow but he was never far away, especially on concert day.

"Yeah." Channing leaned over to look at the screen too. "He was right there near the stage, then he walked off with some guy in a stadium uniform."

"The bus must have turned up," Zeke said, airing my initial thoughts. "But he should be here by now." He looked as worried as I felt.

I glanced at my phone again. Only a minute had

passed. I sighed, then looked over at Zeke, who was draped over a chair, his ankle resting on his opposite knee.

"I'm gonna call Jackson and see where he is." He pulled out his phone and tapped at the screen. He frowned until Jackson's voice came through the line.

"Jackson," Zeke said, his phone to his ear. "Where the hell are you?" He frowned. "Oh, that sucks."

"What?" I mouthed at him.

He waved me to silence. "Well, you should have Hunter there to help you." He listened for a moment. "What do you mean he's not there?"

I sat up in my chair. "What the fuck?"

Zeke waved at me again.

I gave him a dark look, but sat in silence and listened.

"Okay, well where are you then? We can come to — What is that?" Zeke frowned. "Jackson? Jackson?" He pulled the phone away from his face and looked at the screen. "He hung up. Or the call cut out."

"Where is he?" My heart was thundering through my chest. "What did he say?"

"He said the bus broke down," Zeke said evenly. "Hunter never found the bus. I sent him to make sure it got here." He looked at Parker accusingly.

"That was what I was going to tell you," Parker

said. "When he got back to the bus, it wasn't there. He couldn't find it."

"How well does anyone know the bus driver?" Channing asked softly.

"More importantly, what happened to Jackson?" Landon asked.

"Oh my god," I whispered, barely willing or able to voice the words. "You heard something, didn't you? What was it?"

"I don't know," Zeke admitted. "It sounded like a… I don't know, a muffled bang."

"Like a shot from a silencer?" Asher asked.

Zeke glanced towards the bright green carpet on the floor. "Kinda like that, yeah. I can't be sure what it was though. It might be unrelated. Just a random sound in the background."

My heart sank. I swallowed hard. "But you think it was a gunshot, don't you?"

He looked back up. "Yeah, it sounded like that. But let's not jump to conclusions, okay? It could have been anything. It might have had nothing to do with Jackson. He probably ducked, that's why the call ended. He could have—" He shook his head. "I'll try him again." He tapped at the screen and waited, a frown on his face. In spite of telling us not to worry, he obviously was.

So was I. The sound could have been nothing, but it could have been something. Everything. I held my breath and hoped like hell Jackson was okay.

The call ended without being answered.

"Shit," Zeke said softly. He glanced sharply at Parker. "Where the fuck is Hunter?"

"And why the hell didn't you tell us sooner that he hadn't found the bus?" Penn demanded. "And don't say because we didn't ask, or I will rip your motherfucking head off and use it to shoot hoops. Hoops made from your intestines."

"And I'll help," Asher said. "I've always been good at basketball."

Parker shrugged. "Because he's still trying. You guys were busy and I didn't see any point worrying you."

"Too fucking late," Tully said coldly. He looked like he wanted to use his ninja skills on Parker.

I didn't think any of us would stop him. Although, could intestines stiffen enough to be used as a hoop? No, I didn't want the answer to that.

"We need to find Jackson," Landon said. He looked like he was about ready to freak out. "The guy in uniform, he didn't really work for the stadium, did he?"

Channing put a hand on his bicep, and his arm

around him, and gave him a squeeze. "We will find him." He sounded so certain it gave me a small spike of hope.

"He can't have gotten far," I said uncertainly. Channing was right, none of us knew the worker.

"Has it occurred to anyone this is a trick to get us to go somewhere?" Penn said.

"Of course it has," Zeke said. "But I'm prepared to take the risk. We're going to find him and he's going to be fine." Failing at this wasn't an option. But if it was, if anything happened to Jackson, heads would roll. Zeke would spill blood. Shit would get ugly.

"Where do we even begin to look?" I asked.

LA was huge. Even a bus with White Wolf Records written down the side in big letters could be just about anywhere.

Zeke gave me a lopsided smile. "The same way we found your phone in Perth."

"You put a tracker on Jackson's phone," Asher said. He rubbed his hands together and looked gleeful.

"I had to insist, but yes, I did," Zeke said. "He was resistant to the idea, but I didn't give him any choice." He started tapping at his phone again.

"Zeke made me give him his phone so he could

put one on mine too." Penn scowled at the lead singer.

Without looking up, Zeke said, "After what the evil twins did to you, I wasn't taking any chances. But it only works if you take your phone with you when you go places."

"You're a bossy asshole, you know that?" Penn asked him.

Zeke glanced up and grinned. "Hell yeah I am. You should be calling *me* sir."

Penn snorted. "Fuck that."

"That's lame," Parker remarked.

We tried to ignore him, but one by one our gazes turned to him.

The asshole looked as smug as shit.

"What's lame?" Channing snapped.

"Needing a tracker to find people," Parker said.

"You have a better method?" The saxophonist asked. Channing looked interested in spite of himself.

I have to admit, I was curious myself. What sort of skills did these kinds of people actually have?

Parker rolled his eyes. "Of course I do," he said. "But I'm not going to tell you because none of you are interested in joining, or rejoining, the family."

"Where did you put it?" I asked.

He looked at me with his eyebrows half-mast. "I could take that so many ways, beautiful girl, but I'm going to have to ask what you mean specifically."

"The tracker," I said insistently. "Because you're full of shit, and I was unconscious in your company for fuck knows how long. You assholes put one somewhere on me, didn't you?" The idea was disgusting enough to make me physically ill.

Zeke squinted at me. "It's not your phone. There is only room for one in there and it's mine. It's still active." His eyes went to my ears.

Trying not to panic, I put my hands on my earrings and jerked in my seat.

The back of one of them was chunkier than the back of another.

Faster than I ever did anything before in my life, I undid the earring and pulled it out of my lobe. I held it in the palm of my hand. I had to squint, but something was definitely attached to my silver, heart-shaped earring.

"Fucking hell, you piece of shit—" My face hot with anger, I glared at Parker like I might skin him with my eyes. Knowing they did that while I was unconscious, I felt violated all over again, sick to my stomach.

"Here, let me," Zeke said. He reached over and

plucked the earring out of my hand. He squinted at it, then rose and took it out to the corridor, where the floor was hard linoleum. He dropped the earring on the floor and ground down on it with the heel of his shoe.

The crunch of the tracker breaking was satisfying. More so than seeing Zeke destroy my poor earring.

"My grandmother gave me those," I said sadly. They were nothing fancy but they had a lot of sentimental value.

"I'll buy you a new pair," said Tully and Asher at the same time.

I looked over at them and smiled. "That's sweet." No doubt I would be inundated with earrings any moment now, but it wasn't quite the same since my grandmother died a few years ago. It was the thought that counted, I supposed. The guys were sweet like that.

"It's a shame you don't have a clit piercing," Parker remarked. "That would have been more fun to put a tracker in."

No one moved fast enough to stop Penn before he leapt up and drove his fist into Parker's face. The crunch of bone and spray of blood was almost as satisfying as the tracker breaking.

Parker let out a cry of pain and threw a hand up over his nose.

Penn swore under his breath and shook out his fist. "There, now we'll be able to tell you two apart easier. You'll be the one with the crooked nose." He looked around at all of us. "Sorry, did someone else want to do that?"

"Only all of us," Tully said. "But we wouldn't want to deprive you of the privilege."

Penn gave him a smile and a shrug and rubbed his fist with his other hand. No doubt Parker's face was as hard as it looked.

"As much fun as this is, shouldn't we be looking for Jackson?" Channing asked. He looked satisfied at the sight of blood dripping onto Parker's shirt. The sides of his mouth turned up.

"Yes, we should." Zeke looked back at his phone screen. "The tracker is narrowing it down, but there's a lot of interference from," he waved his hand vaguely, "city shit."

"City shit is the worst," Landon agreed. He managed a lopsided smile in spite of the edge of fear in his eyes. He was anxious at the best of times, and this was not of the best of times.

Parker muttered something, but the words were

muffled by the hem of his shirt, which he'd pulled up to dab at his nose.

"No one cares," Penn snarled at him. "Unless you have something useful to say, then shut the fuck up or I'll shut you up."

Parker held up a hand in surrender.

Honestly, I was glad Penn punched him. If he hadn't, I might have. I was going to have nightmares about trackers, and the twins touching me. The thought of what they might have done, and the fact they knew I didn't have a clit piercing, was bad enough. Unless it was a lucky guess. I wanted to believe that, but we didn't call them the evil twins for nothing.

"All in favour of Penn shutting Parker up?" Asher raised his hand. At the same time, he stood. He had his usual smile on his face, but worry in his eyes.

We all raised our hands, but our eyes were on Zeke, waiting for him to give the word. About finding Jackson, not about Penn shutting Parker up. At least, that's what I thought we were waiting for. We might have been waiting for both. I mean, that would be fair enough, but not the priority right now. Maybe later.

He shook his head. "It's narrowed down to a block or two radius. There's too much interference to get a fix on wherever his phone is. Even then, we have to hope he's near his phone."

"This is why trackers in piercings are so much more reliable," Parker said. He ducked away from Penn, who loomed over him. "What? That's useful information. I bet Zeke will do that from now on."

"Be quiet, or I'll shove one up your ass," Zeke snapped. He raised his eyes slightly and made a face. "On second thought, no I won't. I don't need my hand anywhere near your ass." He stood reluctantly. "We'll have to try looking in the area and hope to find him. Come on."

We followed him out the door and down the corridor. Everyone fell into their usual formation, around me. Tully slipped a hand into one of mine and Asher took the other. Usually, that would give me all the comfort I needed, but today…

Today I wouldn't relax until I saw Jackson, alive and well, with my own eyes.

15

CHANNING

"Join a band, they said. It will be fun, they said." I glanced at Landon, who walked beside me. We'd taken up the spot behind Abbie and the other guys.

Parker trailed behind us like a bad smell, dressed in a clean shirt he grabbed from someone in the stadium. He managed to wipe most of the blood off his face, but his nose was swollen. It looked painful.

Good, he deserved it. That and more.

"You're not having fun?" Landon asked. He clearly wasn't either, but he managed to cling to some of his good humour.

"To be honest with you," I said slowly, "I thought we might spend more time playing music and less time running around trying to find people while avoiding being attacked."

If I'd known how this would go, I would have taken the time to kill a few Fiorellis before we left Australia. We could be enjoying our time in LA right now. We could be having lunch in a nice little restaurant by the water. Maybe a couple of beers. We could go swimming in the hotel pool.

But no, I had to go and leave them alive to fuck with us, didn't I?

Yeah okay, I didn't know, but if I had I would have dealt with it. Hell, I would have contended with Zeke and Asher who also would have tried to deal with it, if they knew.

Tully too maybe, even though he hated killing and violence. In spite of that, I'm pretty sure he enjoyed watching Penn punch Parker as much as the rest of us had.

"If you look up, 'rock star,' on the Internet, you'll probably find it involves a lot of playing music," Landon agreed. "And a bunch of interviews, writing songs, recording songs and shit like that. But we're Wolf Venom, we like to change things up."

"We're pretty good at fucking things up too," Asher said over his shoulder.

"Speak for yourself," Penn said.

"I always do," Asher said lightly. "Are we close?" He looked over Zeke's shoulder at the phone screen.

"Closeish," Zeke said. "Keep your eyes open. And before anyone says it, I know we're being followed." He said all of that in the same tone of voice, so I almost missed the last bit.

"Yeah, Parker is behind us," Asher said. He grinned, but clearly knew what Zeke was referring to.

"As long as he stays between us and them." I looked back and gave Parker a dirty look. Let him be killed. I wouldn't lose any sleep over it. In fact, I might throw a party. Was that morbid? Absolutely. Did I give a shit? Hell no. Bring it on.

He smiled at me and waved. "Just in case anyone was in any doubt, I'm not going to die for any of you."

"That remains to be seen," I said darkly. "Sometimes shit happens. Don't worry, we'll make it look like an accident."

Landon looked at me sharply, but I wasn't joking. We had a deal not to kill the twins, but that didn't mean I had to save them if trouble came knocking at their door. I wouldn't rule out cheering their attackers on, before we got the hell out of there.

"Channing," Landon started.

"Don't worry, I'm not going to do anything unless I have to," I assured him.

"I know," he said quickly. "Don't leave us behind this time. We're all in this together. Okay?"

I draped an arm over his shoulders and gave him a sideways squeeze. "Yes, yes we are." I managed a glance back, wide-eyed and looking around like a tourist who was amazed at finding himself in Los Angeles. Yep, we were definitely being followed. They weren't even being subtle about it.

"I get the feeling we're being herded," I said. Like lambs to the slaughter.

"Funny, I get the same feeling," Asher said, not sounding amused.

"So do I." Parker walked closer to the rest of us. "Remember, I'm more of a target than most of you are."

"That's true," I said. "Maybe we should split up. Parker can go one way and the rest of us will go another."

"If I trusted him, I would do that," Zeke said. "I can't rule out the possibility he's involved."

"Come again?" Parker asked. He shook his head and stared at Zeke. He seemed genuinely confused.

"Hunter went looking for the bus, and any potential attackers, and now it and Jackson are missing," Zeke said. "Your girlfriend is from a family that hates ours. You could easily switch allegiance and work against Reuben." He looked at his youngest brother through narrowed, accusing eyes.

"Would that be a bad thing?" Abbie asked. "If Reuben was out of the way, maybe the Bell and Brantley family would get along. They might make peace with the Fiorelli family, then everyone can live happily ever after."

"This isn't a fairytale," Zeke told her. "If they killed Reuben, Caleb would take over. And Joshua after him. Then Lucas after that. By the time they got down to him there would be blood in the streets."

"Unless they took all of them out once," Asher said. He sounded as if he liked the idea.

"Unless that," Zeke agreed. "That would still leave the twins as head of the family."

"Technically, Hunter would be the head," Parker said. "Since he managed to sneak out five minutes ahead of me. Right now, I'm struggling to see a downside to this."

"The downside is you're an asshole," Penn said. "The world doesn't need to give you any more power."

"The world doesn't get to decide," Parker said. "But now the idea is out there, it's something to think about."

"You would never do it," Asher said. "For one thing, it would mean you have to think for yourselves. Two minutes of that and your brains would implode."

"That's hilarious," Parker said dryly. "For the record, we're not working against Reuben."

"Yet," I said. Give it time, they would likely turn on him eventually. He had that way of being an absolute asshole. If I was related to him, I'd probably turn on him too. "I don't know why the Fiorelli family is bothering. They could sit back and watch you all kill each other."

"I'll bring the popcorn," Penn said.

"I'll bring the beer," Asher said. "And vodka for Abbie."

"That's so thoughtful of you," she said. "I'll wear my best little black dress."

"And the black lace bra and panties I like so much?" Asher asked her.

"Sure," she said lightly. "Or better yet, I could wear none."

"None works for me," Asher said. He slid a hand over her perky little ass.

"You know what would suck?" Abbie said.

"Apart from your mouth?" Asher asked.

"Apart from that," she agreed. "What would suck

would be if the Fiorellis killed one of us, when their mission statement is actually not so bad when you think about it. Obviously not the part where they want to kill Zeke too, but the rest of it. I mean, they kind of have a point."

"You're only saying that because you haven't met any Fiorellis," Parker said.

"Or Bells," Asher said. "If you think the Brantleys suck, you ain't seen nothin'."

"The Bells aren't so bad," Parker muttered.

"All I know," Abbie said slowly, "is I've never been kidnapped by anyone from either of those other families. Or anyone with the last name DiMarco." She nodded towards Asher.

"You're welcome," Asher said. "My family has never been into kidnapping. We're more the ones who arranged transport, disposed of evidence and shit like that. We still are, I guess. We also have some renowned assassins in the family. Which I can't tell you about, because, you know, assassins."

"Yeah, I get it," she agreed. "Things don't stay a secret if you talk about them."

"Exactly." He nodded.

I half-listened to the conversation after that. The rest of my attention was on the people following us and the fact we were so good at seeming normal in spite of the fact our manager might be dead right now.

If he was, I was going to blame myself for it. We would all blame ourselves.

It wasn't just his growing relationship with Abbie, or the way he took care of us. He and Levi saw a rough group of guys and knew what we could become. They might say we would have made it anyway, but I didn't believe that. Their faith in us and their ability to nurture talent was what got us through.

From day one, Jackson knew how to handle Landon's insecurities, and my inability to keep still. He took no shit from us, but gave none back. He had a way of getting us to do what he wanted, most of the time, without having to bully or be a dickhead.

As the kind of kid who always got in trouble at school, it would be an understatement to say I had no respect for authority. Until Jackson. He taught me that you can have authority and not feel the need to step on people.

"What are you thinking?" Landon asked.

"I was thinking how lucky we are," I said. "Jackson and Levi have been good to us, you know?"

"Yeah, I know," Landon said softly. "I…don't want anything bad to happen to Jackson."

"Jackson is not going to leave you," I said firmly. "No more than I am. You're stuck with him and the rest of us. Okay, baby?"

I heard him swallow.

"I hope so," he whispered. "When this is over, will you come with me to look for Mum again?"

"I will always come with you when you ask," I said lightly. The last thing I wanted to do was see his mother again, but for him I would do anything. I hoped this time he would get the closure he wanted so much.

He glanced over and grinned. "I know you will. You're the best. You guys are all the best." After a moment he added, "Not you, Parker."

Parker huffed. "You know how to hurt a guy." He touched his face lightly. He was obviously in pain. Good, the more the better.

"I know I do," I said darkly. I wanted to hurt him badly.

"When we've taken care of all of this," Parker said slowly, "if you ask nicely, I might even tell you what we did with the rest of the you-know-what."

"I can't wait," I said sarcastically. Honestly though, it was in my best interest to know that information, in case they decided to use it against me. If they tried, then any deal we made was off, as far as I was concerned. I would kill them without hesitation. I would wrap my hands around their throats and squeeze, and squeeze. They would writhe and kick and their eyes would bulge out, but then they would go slack and the light would go out of their eyes...

I blinked a couple of times to clear that mental image out of my brain. Just thinking about it made my cock hard.

Okay, maybe I hadn't just killed those people just to protect Abbie. Maybe I did it because I wanted to. Because a little bit of me got off on it. Got off on feeling powerful.

Okay, that was fucked up, I admit it, but it wasn't like I killed anyone innocent. I would never hurt a child or a puppy. Especially a puppy. Only sick fucks hurt puppies.

"We're close," Zeke said. He glanced from his phone to the street and back again, a heavy crease in his brow.

We all knew that, if only because the people following us were closer now. The streets were getting quieter, more industrial. The less chance of collateral damage. Less chance we would have somewhere to run and hide. They knew we knew they were there, I could tell in the way they walked. They were confident we knew we were screwed.

Part of me wanted to suggest we all stop and go back to the stadium. Call the cops, let them look for Jackson.

None of us would do it. We'd leave here with Jackson or not at all.

16

ABBIE

"WELL, THERE'S THE BUS," I said rhetorically.

We were herded into a parking area at the back of the building. The bus was parked right in the middle, at an angle across several spaces. I think the expression is, 'As sus as fuck.'

"That is some shit parking if I ever saw it," Penn remarked, as if that was what mattered here. "What if someone else wanted to park here?"

"Just a wild guess," Tully said, "but I think that's the point."

"On a scale of one to a hundred, Levi is going to be really pissed if anything happens to his bus," Asher said. He was squinting, trying to make out if anyone was inside.

"On a scale of one to a hundred, I'm going to be

pissed off if someone doesn't explain what's going on here," Channing said.

"You and me both," Zeke said. "All of you stay back here." He turned and glared at us. "I mean *all* of you. Even you, Parker."

Parker held his hands out to either side. "I have no desire to go any closer to that." He nodded toward the bus. "In fact, I'm going to do you a favour and stay right back here, behind all of you. You know, in case it blows up or some shit."

Penn muttered something about sending Parker on ahead and us staying behind him, but no one paid him much attention.

The people who followed us here, there were only four of them, arrayed themselves behind us. None of them looked like they wanted to get closer to the bus either, but their presence suggested it might not explode. Hopefully.

Zeke walked forward as the door to the bus opened slowly.

A woman stepped out. She was dressed in a long, black pencil skirt and a red silk blouse. Her hair was dark, almost black, and pulled into a neat bun. She looked like a personal assistant in a law firm. Or maybe a lawyer.

"Ezequiel Brantley, I presume," she said smoothly.

She held out her hand, long-fingers with perfect, blood red fingernails.

"Zeke," he corrected. He crossed his arms over his chest and left them there until she lowered her hand.

"I'm Renae Fiorelli." She didn't seem concerned at his rebuff. "You may be aware of the growing tension between your family and mine."

"I'm aware you want us dead," Zeke said, his tone perfectly cool. "You might be aware we have no intention of dying anytime soon. You might also be aware I'm estranged from my family and their business interests."

"And yet, you're in the company of one of your brothers," she pointed out. She gestured towards Parker. The sun glinted off a huge diamond on her hand.

Zeke didn't respond to that. Instead, he said, "Have you seen our manager? We seem to have misplaced him."

She sighed as though he was being rude for not wanting to play into whatever mind fuck she had going.

"I have," she said. "He's perfectly safe. For now."

Before she could add anything else, Zeke said, "Where is he?"

It was her turn to ignore him. "I'd like to offer you a trade. Your manager for your twin brothers."

"Deal," Penn said immediately.

"Hey," Parker protested. "No deal."

Zeke turned around to give them both a look. He turned back and said, "Why should I deal with you at all? Your family tried to kill me back in Perth. Here's a newsflash for you, it wasn't appreciated."

"Because I hold all the cards anyway," she said. "I have your manager and you're surrounded."

"And you're outnumbered," Zeke said evenly. "You have one more person on the bus watching over Jackson. There's eight of us and six of you. And you aren't armed, unless you managed to fit a gun under that tight skirt, or in one of your heels." He looked her up and down, his head sideways. "Also, stilettos are going to slow you down. Right Asher?" He glanced over his shoulder.

"I'm not speaking from experience or anything," Asher said, "but Zeke is right. You ain't going anywhere in those."

"I do have experience, and they're both right," I said. "Luckily, one of us wore sensible shoes to this… Whatever this is." I raised one sneaker-covered foot.

"Are you sure you're not speaking from experience?" Landon asked Asher.

MAGGIE ALABASTER & JO BRADLEY

Asher shrugged and grinned. "That's a story for later. Assuming there is a later."

"There will be," Zeke said. He turned his attention back to Renae. "You haven't shown me proof Jackson is alive."

"She also hasn't said sorry for trying to kill us," Penn pointed out.

"She hasn't, has she?" Asher said. "How rude."

A sliver of annoyance cracked Renae's calm facade.

Look, I'd be the first to admit the guys could be a handful sometimes, but in this case I suspected they were doing it on purpose. If she was angry, she would make a mistake. In theory.

She half turned and waved at someone inside the bus.

A couple of minutes later, Jackson appeared in the doorway, a man behind him with a gun to his head. He looked to be uninjured, but when his eyes flicked to me I saw real fear. Understandable under the circumstances. I would probably pee myself.

"Jackson," Zeke said cheerfully. "It's good to see you. We wondered where you got to."

"Just doing a bit of sightseeing," Jackson said lightly. "Can't say I recommend the tour."

"Maybe next time stick to reputable tour guides," Zeke suggested.

"I think I will," Jackson agreed. "Thanks for the suggestion."

"Anytime, dude," Zeke said. "If you've had enough, how about you step down here and hang out with us?"

"Stay where you are," Renae growled. "I've tried to be reasonable, but my patience is running out." She narrowed dark brown eyes at Zeke.

"That's funny," Penn said, "me too. Hey, Zeke, can we start breaking heads yet?"

"Not yet, Penn," Zeke said. "I'm still considering her offer."

"Bro," Parker complained. "On behalf of Hunter and I, I strenuously object." After a moment he squinted at Renae. "I don't even know where Hunter is right now, do you?"

A flash of uncertainty crossed her features, but she quickly pushed her mask back into place.

"Of course I do," she said smoothly.

"Bullshit," Penn said. "You wouldn't have offered to exchange Jackson for both of them if you already had Hunter in hand. That begs the question, where the fuck is he?" He looked around the parking area meaningfully. Hunter was nowhere to be seen. Knowing him, he was close by, hiding and watching.

Honestly, that's what I'd do if I were him. Actually no, I'd be on a plane to anywhere but here, but I had a sneaking suspicion he wouldn't bail without his twin. Honour amongst assholes and all that.

"Don't twins have telepathy or something?" Tully asked Parker.

"Yeah, but it doesn't include a GPS," Parker said. "I'm pretty sure he's not dead though."

"Shame," Penn muttered.

Channing made a sound of agreement.

"It seems we have a problem," Zeke said. "Even if I wanted to swap Jackson for the twins, I couldn't." He spread his hands to either side of him.

"I'm sure Hunter has a phone," Renae said coolly. "It should be a simple matter of calling him and telling him to come here."

Zeke put a hand to his forehead. "Why didn't I think of that? Let me make the call." He shoved his hand into the pocket of his track pants, but instead of pulling out a phone, he pulled out a gun and pointed it at Renae.

"Looks like you're making all the calls now, babe," Asher said. His hand hovered near his pocket.

"Right?" Zeke said. He gave Renae a sardonic

smile. "You didn't think we would come unarmed, did you?"

"I expected you to be reasonable," she said evenly. "Everyone knows there's no love lost between you and your brothers. I proposed a fair exchange. Honestly, I'm surprised you didn't suggest it yourself." She arched a perfectly shaped eyebrow at him.

She must have some organisational skills if she could arrange all of this shit and still have time for the perfect outfit and makeup. I didn't like her, but I respected her style. Credit where credit is due and all that

"They annoy me, but I mostly don't want them dead," Zeke said.

"Mostly being the key word here," Asher said he moved to stand to the side of the Zeke. "Why try to exchange anyway? What sort of gangsters are you? Most of the ones I've met just take what they want."

"Ones who prefer to avoid bloodshed where possible," Renae said.

"Are you saying you wouldn't kill the twins?" Zeke asked.

"The blood of anyone who works for Reuben Brantley is an exception," she said. "We're not interested in killing anyone else."

"That's great," Zeke said. "Jackson is free to come

down here with us then." He gestured with his other hand for Jackson to step the rest of the way off the bus.

Jackson moved forward slightly, his eyes on Zeke's firearm.

Renae raised her hand to stop him. "I haven't agreed to let him go."

Jackson stopped, his mouth tugged to one side. He looked like a deer caught between two lions, not sure if they'd eat him or each other.

"Consider it a gesture of goodwill," Zeke said. "Like you said, there's no love lost between me and my brothers. Parker is over there, probably with a broken nose. Do you see me taking him to hospital?"

"Good point." Parker gestured towards his face. "This hurts like a bitch." When he spoke, it sounded like he had a blocked nose. Which was basically accurate.

"Sorry, not sorry," Penn said. He opened and closed his hand which looked slightly swollen from the punch. He should get some ice on that before tonight's concert. Although, knowing him, he'd get a kick out of playing through the pain.

"How interesting that you don't get along with your brothers," Renae said. "You're very much like them." She looked at him in disgust.

Zeke pointed the gun at her head. "You want to rethink that assumption?"

"That's the same way I'd react," Parker pointed out.

"You know, maybe I *should* hand him over to you," Zeke said thoughtfully.

"I mean, we're nothing alike," Parker said hastily. "Zeke is the nice brother. The one who would never throw his siblings to the wolves. He is the kind, compassionate one in the family. Fuck knows where he got it from. Maybe he's not really related to us at all."

"I like that theory," Asher said. "Unless he's my brother. Otherwise it totally works for me."

"Me too," Zeke said. "Unfortunately, the family resemblance is too strong. Sorry, babe." He shot Asher a regretful look.

"That's okay, I still love you," Asher said.

Zeke, apparently impatient with the stand-off, said, "Here's how things are going to go. Jackson is going to step down out of that bus and we're going to leave. Nobody has to die here today."

"I'm not leaving here without at least one Brantley brother in my possession," Renae said. "My father won't care which one. He'd prefer the twins, but if it's Zeke, then so be it. We'll take the twins out on some other occasion."

"It's not that I mind being taken out by a beautiful woman," Parker said, "but I have a girlfriend."

"Now you care about that," I said.

"Yeah well," he shrugged. "She's too old for me anyway. She has to be, what, thirty-six?"

"Thirty-two," Renae said coldly. "Hardly old, but that wasn't what I meant when I said take you out."

"We all knew what you fucking meant," Penn said. "This dickhead can't keep his mouth shut." He nodded towards Parker.

"Penn loves me, really," Parker said. "Deep down, he's a big softy. Aren't you Penn?"

"No," Penn said. "Not unless you're Abbie, and you sure as shit aren't."

"He definitely isn't," I agreed. In the corner of my eye, I saw a couple of Renae's people step closer. A ripple of fear passed through me. I moved closer to Channing and Landon.

From one moment to the next, the situation turned from an amicable conversation to a shit storm.

The people to either side of us pulled out guns. The guys grabbed me and pushed me down between them.

"Zeke!" The word was ripped from between my lips.

He half turned and raised his gun.

The man behind Jackson raised his and aimed at Zeke.

A shot rang out through the parking area.

I screamed.

17

ABBIE

I SCREAMED.

Time slowed down.

I cowered between Landon and Channing, their arms around me, heads down.

Jackson threw himself the rest of the way down the steps. He barrelled into Zeke and Renae, knocking them both off their feet.

The shot aimed at Zeke missed him, slamming instead into Tully's foot.

Tully let out a yelp of pain.

"Tull!" Asher shouted. He grabbed the guitarist and they both dropped into a crouch, each with a gun in his hand.

Tully, his mouth twisted in pain, aimed at the gunman on the bus and fired.

Blood blossomed on the man's chest. His eyes widened in surprise before he fell, arms flailing. Time stopped until he hit on the ground with a thud and lay still.

One of the other attackers, a woman with a plait of long red hair, aimed at Penn. Before she could pull the trigger, Zeke, on his back, his upper body off the ground, got off a shot. It hit her squarely in the stomach. She grunted in pain and fired back, but missed by a day or two. She crumbled to the ground, gun slipping from her fingers.

A man built like a brick wall, with arms and legs like tree limbs, pointed his gun at Zeke. He squeezed the trigger.

The lead singer rolled at the last second. The bullet hit the road.

The man hit the ground when Asher shot him in the centre of his chest.

Tully took out the guy with the baseball hat on backwards, one bullet striking him in the knee, another in his wrist when it seemed the man wasn't going to give up.

Baseball Guy gave a shout of pain and dropped his gun. It was Penn who scooped it up and, apparently without thinking, shot the last guy in the groin.

The guy, eyes wide dropped to the ground, hands over his crotch.

"That's gotta fucking hurt," Asher said.

"Sucks to be him." Zeke got to his feet, pulling Renae up with him by her arm. "Kinda sucks to be you too," he told her. "Having your people attack us like that was... What's the word?"

"Dumb as fuck?" Penn suggested. "That's three words, but whatever." He tucked the gun away and crouched beside Tully. The guitarist sat on the ground and pulled off his shoe and sock.

"It's just a graze," Tully winced, his brow scrunched up. "It hurts like fuck though."

"Lucky you don't play with your feet," Asher said.

"Yeah, that's the important thing here," Tully said sarcastically. He grunted as Penn took his sock and wound it around the wound.

"Dumb as fuck works," Zeke said finally. "Is everyone okay?"

"Yeah," Channing said. He drew Landon and me to our feet. "We're fine."

"You definitely are," Landon told him. "I've never seen him move that fast."

"Yeah," I agreed. "I've never been knocked off my feet quite so quickly." I managed a small smile but I was trembling. Five people lay dead or maimed around us. Blood from one of them trickled like a glistening, red creek to the gutter. My stomach turned.

"If it wasn't for Jackson, I would be dead right now," Zeke said. "I guess I owe you a blood debt now or something."

Jackson looked pale and shaky. He stood with his back to the bus, leaning on it for support. "All in a day's work for a manager. No big deal."

I walked over to him and slid my arms around his neck. "It's a huge deal." I pressed my mouth to his in a long, slow kiss. When we stopped to take a breath, I looked at him sternly. "I was worried about you. What did Zeke say about people going off by themselves?" I would have shaken my finger at him, but my arms were busy clinging tight to him. I might not let go.

He smiled slightly. "I was told there was a problem with the bus. I didn't expect it to take this long or be this—" he searched for the right word.

"Entertaining?" Asher suggested. "Interesting? Hair-raising?"

"Fucked up?" Penn suggested.

"Fucked up sounds right," Jackson said. "I see your point about being kidnapped now. It's not as much fun as it sounds."

"I should think not," I said dryly. "It doesn't sound like fun at all, because it isn't. At least it wasn't evil twins this time."

"Speaking of the evil twins," Channing said. "Where are they?"

I glanced around, but sure enough Parker was gone. That might be the first smart thing he did since I met him.

"I don't suppose you put a tracker on him?" I asked.

"No," Zeke said ruefully. "Don't worry, he'll turn up. He always does."

"Like a shit on the bottom of your shoe," Penn said. "No matter how much you wipe, you can't get it off."

"Something like that," Zeke agreed. He turned his attention to Renae. "I hope you realise the smart thing for me to do right now would be to kill you."

"I do realise that," she said. "But that would make the situation worse between our families. Specifically between my family and you. Right now, you're not the enemy. Killing me would change that."

"That's the only reason I'm not going to," Zeke said. He shoved her away from him.

She staggered and almost fell. Heels aren't good for that either.

"I'll tell my father—"

Whatever she was going to say was interrupted by another gunshot and a bullet-sized hole in her forehead. Her eyes widened and mouth dropped open in surprise. She stood for what felt like a year, but it was probably no more than a second or two.

Then she crumpled to the ground like a broken doll.

"Fucking hell," Zeke swore. He spun around to see Hunter standing with a gun in his hand, the barrel aimed where Renae had stood seconds earlier.

"Checkmate." Hunter lowered the gun.

"You fucking idiot," Zeke snarled.

"Yeah," Penn agreed. "It's not checkmate until you've captured your opponent's queen. All you've done is take out one pawn. Anyone with a passing knowledge of chess would know that." He gave Hunter a disgusted look and shook his head.

"Penny's inner geek is alive and well," Asher remarked.

"Penn just thinks you should be accurate if you're going to use chess terms," Penn said. "Otherwise, use terms like bullseye or some shit like that."

"I'll bear that in mind for next time," Hunter said.

"Hunter!" Parker rolled out from under the bus. "That was fucking awesome."

"Park— what the fuck happened to you?" Hunter tucked the gun away and stared at his twin.

Parker grinned and then winced. "Penn happened, but it's no big deal. Just a little love tap."

"He's only saying that because you're outnumbered," Asher said. "Believe it or not, Parker was a dickhead and Penn took exception to it."

"Right." Hunter touched his fingertips to his twin's nose. "That looks painful, bro, but kinda cool."

Parker jerked his face away. "It is painful, bro." After a moment he asked, "Do you really think it looks cool?"

"Totally does," Hunter said. "Lila is going to dig the whole crooked nose thing."

"I'm happy to give you one too," Penn offered. "Although I think it's Tully's turn." He waved towards the guitarist.

Tully held up a hand. "I'm happy to miss my turn. Besides, I think I'd be fighting Zeke for that privilege."

"Hell yeah, you would," Zeke said. To Hunter he said, "What the fuck did you kill her for?"

"Because she would have killed us," Hunter said easily. That seemed to be all the excuse he needed.

"Yeah," Parker agreed. "You didn't really buy all that, 'you're not really our enemy,' shit, did you?

Sooner or later, you're going to end up on the chopping block." He looked over at Channing. "Not literally, like what you do," he said. "I'm speaking figuratively."

Channing stuck two fingers up at him.

"Always charming," Hunter said. "Well, the warmup was interesting. I hate to see what they're going to throw at us for an encore."

"Maybe we shouldn't stick around to find out," Parker said. "This might be a good time to make ourselves scarce."

"The deal is, you help us," Zeke said. He gave Parker a dark look like he was about to shoot his kneecaps off. He must have been tempted. I'd bet anything he wasn't the only one either.

"If they want, they can opt out of the deal," Channing said. "That means we get to do the same thing."

The implied threat should not have been hot, but it was.

I held on to Jackson a little tighter. His body felt hard pressed against mine. Part of me, and not even a small part, wanted him to fuck me up against the side of the bus. Right here, right now, with all those bodies and all that blood…

The sensible part of me remembered the police might turn up any minute now.

Yeah, the sensible part of me was a spoilsport.

Hunter growled. "Fine, we'll stick around, but not for the rest of the day. We're taking the night off and I'm taking Parker to the hospital to have his nose looked at."

"Good, fuck off." Zeke waved him away.

"We should all get out of here," Jackson said. "Luckily the keys are still in the bus."

I leaned my head back and looked at him. "Do you know how to drive a bus?"

He gave me a lopsided smile. "It's not my preferred method of transport, but yeah, I do."

"That's kinda hot," I said.

"You think so?" he asked, his eyebrows high.

"Yeah, I do think so," I said. It wasn't a skill everyone had. To be in control of something that big was kind of sexy.

"Jackson usually rides a motorcycle," Asher said helpfully.

My eyebrows shot up. "Really?"

Jackson shrugged one shoulder. "Yeah, really. An old Triumph Bonneville, to be exact."

"That's very hot," I said. "Will you take me for a ride some time?" Yes, I meant it both ways.

He grinned. "Of course I will." So did he, I saw it in his eyes. He reluctantly unwound me from himself just enough to lead me up the steps into the bus. "Just out of curiosity, what did you think I drove? A Volvo?" He smiled wryly.

I snorted a laugh. "I wouldn't insult you like that." I stood to the side to let the other guys climb onto the bus and watched Jackson start the engine. "Maybe an SUV. But a black one. I'm sure badass people drive black SUVs."

"You think I'm a badass?" he asked.

I leaned down to kiss his cheek. "Hell yeah, boss."

He groaned.

I grinned and went to slip into the seat beside Tully. "How's the foot?"

He flashed me a smile of gratitude. "Hey, loveliness. It hurts, but I'll live. It could have been worse. It could have hit me in the hand."

"Or the groin." I jerked my head towards the window. The man Penn shot was lying still now. As far as I could tell, he was dead.

"That would be bad," Tully agreed. "I need my cock for things. Like fucking our beautiful girl."

"When you put it that way, I need it too," I said. Even after everything that happened, I was so turned on I'd probably come if someone touched my clit with a feather. Which they should totally do, because it sounded like fun.

"I'm glad you do," he said softly.

"I'm going to take us back to the hotel," Jackson said over his shoulder. He turned the huge steering wheel and the bus headed away from the carnage and onto the road. "I'll call the doctor to come and look at Tully there. Then we can all get some rest because you guys have a concert to put on tonight."

"Rest," Channing used air quotes. "Who can rest after all of that?"

"You can try," Jackson said. "A couple of nights here and we'll be the hell out of Los Angeles."

None of us was under the illusion this was over. They were going to come against us at some point and they were going to come hard.

At least this tour wasn't boring.

18

ABBIE

"THAT SHOW WAS EPIC," Landon said. He hadn't stopped smiling since he stepped off the stage. Even during the drive back to the hotel, he was still pumped up.

"Of course it was, you were there," Channing said to him. "And you," he said to me. He put an arm around us both and drew us to him.

On some unseen signal, the other guys went to their room and Jackson went to his, leaving the three of us alone. Maybe it was something the guys arranged in advance or maybe it was the vibe. I'd thought about Channing's date proposal since he made it, so my excitement level was off the charts. The whole day had heightened that.

Death, violence, a rock concert— yeah, I was ready for some intimacy.

"And you," I said. "No one plays the sax like you do."

"And no one plays with my sacs like he does," Landon said, still grinning.

I laughed, low in the back of my throat. "I bet." I ran the palm of my hand over Landon's groin and found him already hard. I did the same to Channing and found a matching erection.

"You don't play them badly yourself," Landon said. He took my hand and tugged me towards the bed.

I grabbed Channing and took him with us. "I've had some practice," I said.

I dragged the zip down on the front of Landon's jeans and tugged them down far enough to release his cock.

He twisted his upper body to do the same to Channing.

Both of us took a handful of cock and worked them up and down a few times.

Landon took a step back and lay on the bed. He took me and Channing down with him.

They both shed their jeans and boxers, then sat up.

Almost in unison, they grabbed the hems of their shirts with one hand and pulled them off over their heads. They dumped them on the floor on the opposite sides of the bed.

"You're overdressed there, gorgeous girl," Channing said.

I glanced down at myself. "You're right. What are you going to do about it?"

They both grinned and descended on me, helping me out of my skirt, pale pink T-shirt and white lacy bra and panties.

"That's better," Channing said. He looked me up and down and then pressed me back to the mattress. "I made a promise to you. Wait there for a sec." He climbed off the bed and went over to his suitcase.

Landon watched him with interest for a moment, then rolled over so his upper body was lying over the top of mine, his hand pressed lightly to my hip. He slanted his mouth over mine and kissed me, quick and hungry. His lips and tongue and teeth devoured mine.

"That's a hell of a view," Channing said. He knelt on the edge of the bed and crawled over to us. In one hand, he held a small knife.

I felt Landon grin against my mouth before he pulled away.

"You're a pretty fucking awesome view too, baby," Landon told him. He sat up and snaked an arm around Channing's neck, pulling him in for a kiss.

"*That's* what I call an awesome view," I said. Watching two, muscular, tattooed rock stars kiss each other was just about the hottest thing going. I would never get tired of seeing it. It didn't matter whether it was Landon and Channing or Asher and Zeke, it got me going every time. Especially when their tongues tangled.

I reached down and started to trace circles around my clit with the tips of my fingers. I closed my eyes and savoured the way it felt to touch myself while listening to the wet smacking sounds of their lips on each other's.

I was so lost in that space I didn't notice they stopped kissing until Channing said, "Why don't you let us do that?"

I opened my eyes as he grabbed my wrist and pulled it over my head.

"Keep it there," he said. "And this one too." He pulled my other wrist up to the first. "Don't move them from there, okay?"

"Landon—"

"I have an idea." Landon scrambled off the bed and over to his suitcase. He came back with a brightly coloured tie, covered in animated characters from some anime I wasn't familiar with.

"I like this idea," Channing said.

"Me too," I agreed.

Landon wound one end of the tie around my wrists and bound them together firmly enough that I couldn't spread them apart, but not so tight it hurt. He tied the other end around a lamp that stuck out the side of the headboard.

He leaned back to admire his handiwork. "Perfect," he said. "Are you feeling good, Princess?"

"Yeah," I said. I was tied to the bed between two hot guys, one with a knife in his hand. What could be better? "I'm doing fabulous."

"Can you roll over onto your stomach?" Channing asked.

"I think so." It was awkward with my hands above my head, but I managed it with a shuffling of hips and knees.

"Good girl," Channing said. "I've heard a rumour you enjoy being spanked."

I turned my head to the side and said, "I think you've seen for yourself I do."

"That's true, I have," he said. "You've been smacked by a hand and paddled by a paddle. But now I'm going to smack you with this." He held the knife where I could see it.

"Bring it on," I said. A thrill of fear passed through me. I knew he knew what to do with a knife: how to kill and how not to kill. I knew he had no intention of hurting me. I was also acutely aware of the things he had done. So aware, I was desperate for someone to touch me. I wanted, needed, a cock inside me. If this went on much longer, I might come without a touch.

Channing sat beside my hip and smacked the blade of the knife lightly on my ass. It was cold and hard, and delivered a slight sting.

Landon lay down beside me, his face a few centimetres from mine. "I think she liked that."

"Yes, she did," Channing said. He smacked the blade down, harder this time.

The sting made me wriggle my ass in a combination of pleasure and pain.

"You want to try?" Channing offered Landon the knife.

Landon shook his head. "No thanks, I'm happy to watch her enjoy herself." He ran his fingertip down the side of my face and across my jaw. "So beautiful," he whispered.

"So are you," I said.

Channing smacked me again several times, each increasingly harder. The pain became more intense with each strike.

"Your ass turns a lovely shade of red," Channing remarked. He leaned over and pressed the side of the knife very lightly to my skin. If he twisted it just so, he would slice me open.

He didn't. He pressed the cool metal to me, then lifted it up and traced a line up my back to my shoulders. His slight touch didn't break my skin, but the sensation sent lava hot heat right to my core.

A killer with a knife in his hand was scary, but his control was absolute. He was as skilled with it as he was with his saxophone.

"Roll over onto your back." Channing sat up to give me room.

Landon helped me roll, then moved down to where he could flick his tongue over my nipples.

Channing, kneeling on the other side of me, ran the tip of the knife down my cheek and onto my neck.

I failed to resist the urge to swallow hard.

He stopped. "Do you trust me?"

"I trust you," I said without hesitation. I knew without a shadow of a doubt he would never turn a knife on me. "I love you," I added.

"I love you too." He leaned forward to kiss me briefly, then continued to run the tip of the knife over my neck and across my throat.

I was trying not to tremble now, but it wasn't with fear. It was pure, undiluted need to fuck.

Landon moved away from sucking my nipples and kissed his way down my belly before lying with his face between my thighs.

"I'm going to keep the knife here," Channing said. He pressed the blade to the side of my neck, just below my chin. "You're going to want to buck and wriggle, but don't. And don't come until I tell you to."

I could barely breathe, much less move, but I managed to say, "Okay."

Landon hooked his arms under my legs and opened me out to him. He flicked his tongue over my clit and down to the entrance of my pussy. "She's so wet," he said, sounding very pleased with the discovery. "She definitely likes this."

He started to slowly devour me with his mouth, tasting and teasing.

His touch on my pussy was exactly what I needed. I was on the edge of coming after only a few laps. I headed fast to the crest of the wave but before I got there, he pulled his mouth back.

I groaned. Then again when I felt the edge of the knife prickle my skin.

"Keep still," Channing ordered.

I murmured something incoherent even to myself. Probably a sound of agreement, but frustration at the same time.

Landon lowered his face back to me now that I was no longer right at the edge of the cliff. He lapped at me and slid a finger inside me.

I moaned again. Keeping still was getting more and more difficult. I wanted to roll my hips, beg him to bury his whole hand inside me. I wanted to throw my head back and scream so loud the whole city heard me.

Instead, I kept still as Landon slid another finger inside me. Pressure built faster than a bullet leaving a gun. Before it could pass out of the barrel, Landon pulled away again.

This time, I growled at him.

"Keep still," Channing insisted.

"I can't," I said.

"Yes you can," he said. "And you will."

I bared my teeth at him but he chuckled. Asshole.

"Landon, you can make her come now."

"With pleasure," Landon said. He lowered his face for the third time and hooked his hand around so his fingers were massaging my G spot while his tongue teased my clit.

Pleasure came in an even bigger rush this time. I had to grit my teeth to keep myself still while my body was thrown over the cliff and into the hot, rushing sea of a mind-blowingly intense orgasm. When my back wanted to arch, I had to keep it stiff. When I wanted to shout, I had to grit my teeth harder. The only thing I knew in the world was the most beautiful symphony of sensation and the sharp prick of the blade at my throat.

I stayed up in that place for an eternity. I left my body for at least eight or nine minutes before floating back in a haze.

"Holy fuck," I whispered. "That was…"

"Yeah," it was." Channing took the knife from my throat and tossed it onto the table beside the bed.

He untied my arms and rubbed my wrists to make sure the blood was flowing through.

Landon lifted his face, glossy with my juices. He and Channing exchanged a look before he scrambled off the bed and over to his suitcase. He came back a minute later with a tube of lube in his hand.

"Lie down," Channing told Landon.

Without hesitation, Landon did as he said.

Channing all but picked me up and rolled me so I

was lying face down on Landon, my legs on either side of his hips.

"Hey." Landon grinned up at me.

"Hey." I lowered my mouth to his to kiss him. His mouth tasted of me, sweet and salty.

Channing snapped open the lid of the lube. "We're going to need a lot of this."

A ripple of excitement passed through Landon and he kissed me more deeply.

I felt the cool of the lube on Channing's fingers as he smeared it over and around the entrance to my already wet pussy. I thought I had some idea what he had in mind, but I swallowed deeply anyway.

"Lift your belly up for a minute," Channing said. When I did, he smeared a whole bunch of lube on Landon's cock. Then a bunch on his own.

"Okay, lower yourself onto him," Channing said. "And lean forward."

I did as he asked, closing my eyes and impaling myself on Landon's thick length.

"Lean forward a little further," Channing said. He straddled Landon's legs right behind me and placed his hands on my waist. His erection bumped my ass, before he positioned himself outside my pussy.

Slowly, he pushed the tip inside, sliding along the length of Landon's cock and stretching my pussy.

"Don't tense up," Landon said.

I nodded and tried to relax. With two cocks inside my pussy, that was easier said than done. I swallowed and focused on my breathing, and the feel of being so incredibly full.

After a minute or two, I managed to relax, and Channing pushed himself a little deeper.

"Oh my god," I whispered. I'd fucked some guys with big cocks before, like all of the guys in the band, but never two at once. It was incredible to feel so full.

"Are you okay, gorgeous?" Landon asked.

"Better than okay," I said. I could barely think straight, and that was all right. Thinking was over-rated sometimes. This was all about feeling.

"Are you okay?" I managed to ask. He'd be feeling the pressure too.

"Oh, fuck yeah." He looked blissed out. "If I die now, I'm gonna die happy."

Channing rumbled with laughter. "Don't die now, baby. I can feel Abbie's pussy and your cock and it feels pretty fucking amazing. I'm going to try to get in a bit deeper."

"Do it," I said.

When I thought I couldn't stretch any more, I

did. He was almost all the way in now. Enough I could roll my hips and slowly ride them both.

"Holy fuck," Channing whispered. He made an unintelligible grunting sound, which I interpreted to mean he was enjoying himself too.

"Mmm, I can't even," Landon said. He rocked his hips just slightly, thrusting into me and sliding along Channing at the same time.

"Fucking hell," Channing muttered. "I knew you'd feel incredible. Both of you together is next level."

Landon thrust a little faster. "I'm going to come."

I thought Channing might tell him to wait, but he didn't. Honestly, I don't think he could have held on if he tried.

Or Channing for that matter.

They both moved with short, quick thrusts and then came almost in unison.

A moment later, I came again. I was full already, I became fuller still with two doses of hot cum, mingled in with my own.

The whole world was full of wet heat, panting and fireworks of pleasure. Who knew being stuffed fuller than a Christmas turkey would feel so good?

The guys, obviously. It didn't take a genius to realise they'd done this before. Like every other time I had that thought, I didn't let it worry me. There was no jealousy for any women in their pasts. Or men in their pasts for that matter. The only important thing was here and now, and us. And the way it felt to fall in a heap on the mattress with two amazing, loving guys.

The only thought my tired, extremely relaxed mind could think was, 'how long until we can do that again?'

19

CHANNING

"HEY," Abbie said softly.

Landon was still asleep when I woke, him on one side, Abbie on the other.

After three days in Los Angeles, we were finally almost ready to head to Vancouver. A glance at the clock on the wall showed we had a couple of hours before the tour bus would turn up to collect us. Fortunately, the Fiorellis had only forced the driver off at gunpoint and left him alive. Otherwise, Jackson would have driven us over the border. Or he would have organised someone else to do it.

Whatever, as long as we got there.

"Hey," I said back. "How are you feeling this morning?" We'd basically monopolised her for the last few nights. Judging by the sounds coming from the shower yesterday morning, no one was missing out.

"Good," she said. "You?" She seemed worried Landon and I were going to have squashed cocks from sharing her, but her beautiful pussy stretched to take us both in, like the magical creation it was.

Just thinking of that and being here with her made me hard. I rolled over and straddled her hips, my hands to either side of her face. I kissed her long and slow and deep. Her mouth always tasted amazing. Very quickly, my balls were heavy, my cock aching to be inside her.

I glanced over at Landon as his eyes opened slowly.

I smiled. He was so adorable when he was half asleep.

"Do you want to—" I started.

"If it's okay, I'd like to watch." He covered a yawn with his hand.

"Of course you can." He usually preferred to be watched, but sometimes he liked to lie back and enjoy the show. I was happy to give him one.

I gently pried Abbie's legs apart with my knees.

She raised her knees and let me sink my eager, thirsty cock into her body. She felt amazing with Landon inside her too, but she felt just as incredible when it was just me. All warm and wet and soft. The perfect sheath for my sword. I could stay like this all day.

I slipped my hand between us and rubbed her clit as I thrust slowly. I loved the way she melted underneath me. The way my body pinned her to the bed. In this moment, she was all mine, her beautiful face, her gorgeous body. She belonged to me and Landon. No one and nothing could come between us.

Her breath came in soft little moans.

I glanced around for the knife, to enhance the experience. I thought I'd put it on the table beside the bed last night, but I couldn't see it now. It must have fallen off. I wasn't going to get out of her or off her to find it. Instead, I watched her face and rubbed harder. I could tell she liked what I was doing. She was close to coming.

I looked over at Landon. He'd pushed back the covers and wrapped his fingers around his own cock. Fuck, that was cute *and* hot.

I wanted to edge her, but just this once, I would let her finish quickly.

She must have sensed what I was thinking, because she looked at me like she thought I would take my hand away from her at any moment.

I leaned down to whisper in her ear, "You can come. Come for me, gorgeous girl."

"Only if you come for me, gorgeous boy," she whispered back.

I took my hand off her clit and slid out of her long enough to roll her over and pull her up on to all fours. Then my cock was back inside her and my hand rubbed harder.

At this angle, the piercing on my tip would work her G spot, while my fingers worked her clit and slid through her folds.

"Oh my god," she moaned. "Yes, just like that." She arched her spine and her head rolled back until she touched my hand which rested on her shoulder.

She rocked her hips back onto me, setting a fast pace for us both. Her breath came in little pants, until finally she let out a long, slow groan and ground against me.

I couldn't stop myself if I tried. A warm tingling thunder of pleasure gripped me like a noose. Pressure built until it was all I could feel before I exploded hard and fast inside her. Everything from my stomach to the tip of my cock tingled and sang. I struggled to contain a shout by biting down on my tongue.

Finally I sagged over her and we tumbled down to the mattress, side by side, sweating and puffing.

Landon grunted and came all over his hand, cum dripping from his fingers to the sheets.

"Oh, yeah," I said softly. "That was nice."

"Only nice?" she asked teasingly.

"Better than nice," I said. "It was fucking awesome."

"That's more accurate," she said. She reached over and picked up her phone from the table beside the bed. She turned on the screen and grimaced. "I need to have a shower before we get out of here. I'm sticky."

"You're welcome," I said smugly. I let her go and retreated back to the middle of the bed. That gave me a good view of her naked body as she rose. Most of her skin was smooth and flawless, unlike us guys, who had tattoos wherever we could fit them. I wondered if I could talk her into getting my name inked on her somewhere. And the rest of the guys' too, I supposed. Definitely Landon's.

I couldn't resist wolf-whistling at her before she disappeared into the bathroom. She flashed me a smile over her shoulder and, a moment later, the water came on.

I rolled over to face Landon. He was lying there watching me, looking as adorable as always.

"Good morning, baby." I scooted over to kiss his mouth.

"Good morning. That was awesome, thank you," he said.

"Any time." I dipped the tip of my finger into the cum still on his hand and traced circles around his skin with it. "I'm glad you liked the show."

"I liked it a lot. Seeing you with her is... I don't know. I could watch all day." After a moment, he added, "Okay, *some* of the day. I want to join in for some of it. Lots of it."

I gave him a slow smile. "Did you know, you're the absolute best boyfriend on the face of the planet? I'm so fucking lucky to have you."

"That's funny, I was going to say the same to you," he said. He kissed me, but I sensed he was holding something back.

"Are you sure you're okay?" I asked. "You're not just saying that because you think I want to hear it?"

Before he could answer, someone knocked on the door between our rooms once, twice, then it opened. Zeke stuck his head inside.

"Time to get up, boys and girls," he said. His hair was damp and his face was pink, like he just got out of the shower himself. He must have been up early for some reason. I always knew he had a screw loose.

"We have time for breakfast before we get picked up," he added. "Up you get, lazy bones."

I leaned over the side of the bed and scooped up the first thing I touched to throw at him. It happened to be one of Landon's shoes. It hit the wall beside his head and bounced off.

"We're awake," I said. "Fuck off and let us get up."

Zeke knelt and picked up the shoe before throwing it back at me. It hit the wall behind the bedhead and fell onto the pillow beside Landon's face.

Zeke grinned. "He shoots. He scores!" He danced back out the doorway into the other room.

"He's a fucking idiot," Landon shouted after him, but he was also smiling. It didn't quite reach his eyes.

"I suppose we better get up," I said reluctantly. I rolled off the bed. Landon followed.

I didn't even see him move, but the next thing I knew I was pressed to the wall, my back against the plaster. Landon had the knife in his hand. He put it to my neck.

I raised my hands. "Okay, this is different, but I like it." He wasn't usually the aggressive one, but if he wanted to play like this, I was all in.

"I need you to be honest with me," he said. From the expression on his face, he wasn't playing.

"Always," I said. Fuck, what had they done to make him think I wasn't? Was he actually pissed off about me fucking Abbie after all? This was a violent reaction to it if he was.

"Landon." Abbie must have finished the shower and stepped back out into the room. "What the fuck?"

"What do you want to know, baby?" I asked, my eyes on his. If there was one thing I'd learnt in life, it was never take your eyes off the person with a knife to your throat.

"Did you kill my mother?" He asked. His eyes begged for the truth.

I blinked. "No," I said firmly. "I did not kill your mother."

A flicker of uncertainty crossed his features. "You killed those people to protect Abbie. Why not her?"

"Are you jealous because I didn't kill for you?" I asked. That was all kinds of adorable.

He looked even more uncertain. "No?" He frowned. "I just—"

"I thought about it," I told him. "I didn't because it's not in your best interests. You want to make up with her. I wasn't going to take that away from you.

It's something you need to do. If it wasn't, I would one hundred percent have killed her."

We could have been talking about the weather, or whether or not pineapple belongs on pizza. Somehow killing became an average part of our lives.

He nodded slowly. "Okay, I get it." He lowered the knife until it went slack on his fingers.

I took it from him. "You didn't need a knife to get the truth from me. All you needed to do was ask."

He lowered his eyes. "I know. I wasn't sure if…"

"If I would be honest?" I asked. That actually stung. "You think I'd lie to you?"

"You had a whole other life I knew nothing about," he said. "I'd call that a lie, wouldn't you?"

"Yeah, I guess so," I admitted. "I'm sorry, babe. I was trying to protect you and everyone else. I'm sorry if I didn't go about it the right way."

I handed the knife to Abbie when she hovered over closer. She took it and put it on the table over to the side of the room, then crouched beside her suitcase to grab out clothes and get dressed.

I reached for Landon's hand. For a moment I thought he wouldn't let me take it, but then he did.

"You and I have been through a shit load of things together," I said. "Your mother, my family, the band,

Zeke's family. It's a long fucking list. But at the end of the day, you and I, we're solid. I promise you, I will never lie to you or keep anything from you ever again." I held out my pinky finger.

He looked at it for a moment before hooking his around it. "I believe you," he said. We shook and stayed like that for a while.

Finally, he said, "So, you liked the knife, huh?"

I grinned. "Yeah, that was kinda hot. It's a side of you I've never seen before. It was sexy as fuck."

He blushed slightly, adorably.

"Are you guys okay?" Abbie asked. She was dressed now in a cute little hot pink dress that matched her fingernails. It made her look both younger and sexier at the same time. Like a hot doll.

"Yeah, okay," I said. I looked over at Landon. "Aren't we?"

My heart stopped when he didn't respond immediately, but then he said, "Yeah. Yeah, we are. We all are." He held out his other pinky finger to Abbie.

After a moment, I did the same. She hooked her pinkies in ours and we all shook.

"For the record," she said, "can you warn me if you're going to pull a knife on each other? After everything that's happened, I wasn't sure if—"

"I would never hurt Channing," Landon said. "No

matter how mad I got at him."

"You wouldn't hurt me, but would you kill me?" I asked only half teasing.

"Only if you needed me to," he said. His expression turned sad. "If you couldn't live any more, I would help you."

"I would do the same for you," I said. Fuck, this conversation got dark and morbid. Still, it was good to know we had each other's backs if pain had us but death hadn't taken us yet.

"We would all do that for each other," Abbie said. "That's stuff family does if it can, doesn't it?"

"Yes," I agreed. "And any time either of you need my organ, you only have to ask." I grinned slyly.

They both squeezed my pinky until they hurt, and laughed at the expression on my face.

"We will never not need your organ," Landon said. "It's one of our favourite parts of you."

"Along with the rest of you," Abbie agreed.

"Right back at you both," I said softly. They really were the best fucking people in the world. And I was one lucky fucking saxophonist.

"Let's go, people," Zeke shouted from the other room.

"Yes, General Brantley," I shouted back. Landon and I scrambled to get dressed.

20

ABBIE

"O, CANADA," Asher said as we crossed the border.

Penn scrunched up the empty paper from his ham and cheese sandwich and threw it at Asher's head. It hit him in the cheek and bounced off.

"What the fuck was that for?" Asher demanded.

Penn shrugged. "Because you say that every time we enter Canada."

"I like being consistent, okay?" Asher sneered at him playfully.

"How about you be consistently less annoying?" Penn suggested.

"It's like being on the school bus, isn't it?" I asked Jackson as I curled up against his side.

He grunted. "Yeah, but I don't remember signing up to be the teacher."

"It was right about when you signed up to be our manager," Asher said helpfully. "I'm pretty sure there's a clause in there that included you being the designated adult."

"I knew I should have read the fine print." Jackson grimaced and rolled his eyes, but he smiled the whole time.

"Always read the fine print," I said. "Although, I did and it didn't stop me from being screwed over." Thinking about Pete and Onyx Riot Records would always leave a bad taste in my mouth.

"I would suggest you only sign with people you can trust," Jackson said, "but if that clause is in there, then clearly I was wrong to trust Levi."

"I might make it a stipulation of any contracts going forward with my label," Tully said thoughtfully.

"What? That someone has to be the designated killjoy?" Landon asked.

"That's already in Penn's contract," Zeke said.

Penn flipped him off. "No it's not, I just enjoy being the voice of reason around here. Someone has to be." He shot Jackson an accusing look.

"When am I not the voice of reason?" Jackson asked. "I'm pretty sure that *is* in my contract. Spoilsport, voice of reason, adult and all around badass."

"That sounds accurate," I snuggled in closer. It was nice to get the chance to sit with him. He usually sat by himself like he was the designated nerd on a bus full of cool kids. Although, we were all self-confessed nerds anyway. Maybe that made him the cool kid, keeping us at arm's length.

He squeezed my shoulder. "I'm starting to feel like everyone thinks I'm older than I really am."

I was hoping for that opening, so I took it. "How old are you?"

He hesitated for a moment. "Thirty-six."

"So, definitely not old," I said. Twelve years older than me, but what was age anyway? Just a bunch of numbers.

"You haven't run away screaming yet," he pointed out.

"There's not really anywhere to run," I said. "I could run up the aisle, but there's only two seats behind us. It wouldn't be very satisfying."

His body rumbled with laughter. "In that case, you haven't gotten up and gone to sit somewhere else with a guy closer to your age."

"Because I don't care about age," I said firmly. "I care about *you*."

"I care about you too," he said softly. "For the record, I don't care that you're younger than me."

I looked up at him. "It hadn't occurred to me that you might. Don't guys usually dig dating younger women?"

His eyebrows twitched upward slightly. "I suppose they do. I was going to say I wasn't into that, but maybe I am and didn't know. Whatever, none of that shit matters to me."

We fell silent for a couple of minutes until I broke it by asking, "Do you want to talk about your ex-wife?"

His brow creased, then increased. "If you like. What do you want to know?"

"What happened?" I asked. "You said it didn't work out?"

He sighed. "She married a man with a bad case of the travel bug. First it was touring, then it was managing. She wanted to stay home and have babies. I wanted to see the world."

"You don't want babies?" I asked.

"I don't know," he said thoughtfully. "I didn't back then. I wasn't even in my thirties. I'd only just given up on the dream of making it as a muso. I wasn't ready to hang up my passport yet. I'm not old-fashioned enough to think a child can't be raised by one parent and be happy and healthy, but I think if you bring a child into the world and you're still together, you should see each other once in a while."

I snorted softly. "Yeah, I guess so, but it works for military people. You know what they say, as long as you want to make it work, you can."

"Right," he said so softly I almost missed it. "I didn't want it badly enough. Not with Carla. She was everything the people I spend all day everyday with weren't. Nine to five job, normal home life, pet dog, the ability to keep potted plants and goldfish alive. I thought I wanted something different. I thought I could fit her into my life. Turns out I need someone who gets this life. Who understands the sacrifices we've all made to be here. She never got why I wanted to keep playing and touring, or being around bands. Giving that up would be like..." He thought for a moment. "Giving up breathing."

"I can't imagine you giving any of this up," I said, waving around the bus with one hand. "Unless you get tired of being held at gunpoint, shot at, kidnapped..."

"That part I'm happy to give up," he said. "I could live without that shit in my day."

"When did you find out about the guys and all of that?" I asked. "I mean, that's not the usual thing that comes up in conversation. Does it?"

"Not really," he agreed. "Zeke didn't just walk up one day and say, 'Hey, dude, my family are gangsters.' Although, that might have made life easier." He glanced back in Zeke's direction.

"Hey, dude," Zeke protested. "That would have gone down like a lead fart, wouldn't it?"

"Not really," Jackson said. "I wouldn't have believed you."

"Yeah, there you go, that's why I didn't tell you," Zeke said.

"So, how did you find out?" I pressed. "Was it the evil twins or Reuben?"

"Actually, it was Caleb," Jackson said. "He took it upon himself to ask if I could help smuggle things over the border. When I asked Zeke about it, he admitted what was going on."

"Caleb was trying to stir up shit," Zeke said darkly. "He was lucky I didn't put his nose down his throat until it came out his ass." After a moment he added, "No, that's not completely accurate. He also wanted you to smuggle shit. Wanted us to do it. If we had, he might have gone to bat for us with Reuben, to get him to back off a bit. On the other hand, I don't want to spend the rest of my life in a jail cell somewhere on the other side of the planet, so…"

"Wow," I said. "That was really bold of him to

approach you like that. Did he not think you would call the police?"

"And tell them what?" Jackson asked. "His suggestion was less direct than that and I had no proof he made it in the first place. It would have been his word against mine and the world mostly knows Caleb Brantley as a reputable businessman."

Penn snorted loudly. "Reputable, my ass."

"Yeah, well," Jackson shrugged, "it would have created a shit storm and Zeke would have been stuck in the middle of it. And me too. No doubt the Brantley family is perfectly capable of fabricating some shit to make me look like I was the bad guy."

"Without a doubt," I agreed. They wouldn't have cared if Jackson spent the rest of his life behind bars for something they did. "That must have freaked you the fuck out."

"It was disconcerting," Jackson agreed. "But they understood quickly we weren't going to do what they wanted."

"That was right around the time Reuben started to badger Zeke about going back to the family," Asher said. "If he couldn't get to him via Jackson or the label, then he would go direct."

"Hey, Channing," Penn said suddenly. "How come you didn't kill Reuben?"

We all turned and looked at Channing.

He shrugged. "Because I wouldn't get out alive if I did that. I'd have to take out his minions as well. Don't worry, I did think about it."

"I can't believe I'm saying this," Zeke said, "but I'm glad you didn't. That would have made a shitty situation a whole lot shittier. You would have had all of our brothers, and Damon and Gianni, his most loyal minions, after your ass. Things wouldn't have ended well for you."

"Says you," Channing said. Before Zeke could respond, he added, "As it happens, I agree with you. I like my balls where they are, not shoved down my throat."

"The only balls he wants in his mouth are mine," Landon said helpfully.

"Exactly," Channing agreed. "I'm a one set of balls kind of guy."

I smiled at them both. I was glad he hadn't killed Reuben too, if only because I would have missed out on meeting him. Channing that was. I could live without having ever met Reuben.

Since Landon was always with Channing, the bad guys might have taken him out too. What would Wolf Venom be without its rhythm guitarist and saxophone player? Much less wolfie and venomous, that was for sure.

That begged another question. I seemed to have a lot of them today.

"Where did the name Wolf Venom come from?"

"Zeke and Asher came up with it," Landon said.

Asher nodded. "We thought of the two coolest things we could think of and put them together. What could be cooler than wolves and venom?"

I pretended to think about that for a moment "I can't think of anything. Although, you could have blended your names like Blazing Violet did and been Ashing Zeke, or Zekeing Ash." I held back a grin.

"The first thing that Levi would have insisted on is them changing their name if they went with either of those," Jackson said. "No offence though."

I sniffed. "Offence totally taken." Okay, they were silly suggestions, but they weren't without their charm. "Luckily I did better with my own name."

They all turned and looked at me funny.

I looked from one face to the next. "What? You didn't think my last name was actually Hart, did you?"

"Ummm…" Asher said.

"I did," Landon said. "What is it?

Penn groaned. "Please say it's not Brantley, DiMarco, Bell or Fiorelli. Or Pennington."

"I'm surprised you don't know what it is," Channing said to him.

"I know this will come as a shock to you, but I don't know everything." Penn sneered at him.

"No shit," Channing said.

"So, what is it?" Landon pressed. He frowned briefly. "I bet Jackson knows."

Jackson shrugged one shoulder "I might. It is my job to know stuff like that."

Everyone but him looked at me speculatively.

"It's Sharp," I said finally. "Can you imagine a muso going through life with the name A Sharp? It was bad enough at school when the other kids would ask if I was a sharp minor or major." It was funny now, but at the time it drove me crazy.

"I like Hart better," Landon said. "It describes you perfectly. You have a big heart."

I gave him a soft look. "Awww, thank you. That's very sweet of you. I don't know about that but A Hart sounds better to me than A Sharp."

"It's perfect." Jackson kissed the top of my head and I melted a little more. It was nice to forget all the trouble for a little while.

If only I didn't have a nagging feeling that the closer we got to Vancouver, the closer we came to being completely fucked.

Not in a good way.

21

ABBIE

"I'm starting to feel like I could do sound checks in my sleep," Asher remarked.

"If you can't by now, then you might be in the wrong profession," Jackson said dryly.

"Was that a burn?" Asher asked him.

"If you can't recognise a burn by now, you're definitely in the wrong profession, babe," Zeke teased.

"Hold me," Asher said to me, a playful, pained expression on his face.

I gave him a hug, then a shove toward his drums. "You're a big boy, you can take it."

He turned around and grinned. "Can I ever."

"Everything is about sex with these guys," I complained to Jackson.

He draped an arm over my shoulders and tucked me into his side. "Yes, and?"

I snorted a laugh. "You're as bad as they are."

He grinned unapologetically. "It's not my fault. I was sweet and innocent before I met them."

"That is such bullshit," Penn said. "The only innocent one around here is—"

"Shhh," Zeke urged.

"What—" Penn asked.

Zeke made a zipping gesture with his fingers across his lips.

We all froze.

Jackson's hand tightened over my shoulder. He wanted to ask what it was, I saw that on his face, but when it came to matters of our safety and security, he always deferred to Zeke.

I looked around the empty stadium, but saw nothing but vacant seats and tour staff moving around fixing the rigging, adjusting lights and speakers. Nothing seemed out of place.

In spite of that, the hairs on the back of my neck rose. I might have put it down to me reacting to Zeke's sudden, wary expression, but he wouldn't look like that unless something was really wrong.

"Everyone off the stage," Zeke said. He gestured

to us, but not to the stairs at the back. Instead, he waved us towards the seats.

"What's going on?" Asher whispered as he moved silently past Zeke.

"I dunno." Zeke shook his head. "It might be nothing but go."

We stepped or jumped off the stage.

Jackson jumped down in front of me, then turned to take my hand and help me down. If this was a performance, I would have been wearing heels. When it came to the sound check I took the advice I gave to Renae and wore sensible shoes. The rubber soles only made a slight thud as I hit the ground. That still made me wince.

"Where to now?" I asked Zeke.

Before he could respond, a sound came from backstage.

It sounded like a gunshot, echoing through the corridor.

"Fuck," I said under my breath.

We didn't wait for Zeke to give us any further orders, we all bolted as silently as we could into the seats.

Following Tully's lead, I stayed as low as I could and crept up through the tiers. I trusted the guitarist's instincts as well as I trusted Zeke's. A trained assassin would know how to stay out of sight.

By the time this was over, if it was ever over, I would have an interesting skill set, if not a marketable one by reputable standards.

The higher I got, the darker it was, but I saw Tully wave me over to him.

I glanced toward the stage, then slipped over as quickly and quietly as I could.

I dropped into the space beside him as footsteps sounded on the steps leading up from backstage.

"They're getting desperate," Tully whispered in my ear. "Coming after us here is…"

"Crazy?" I suggested. I startled as Penn appeared on the other side of me.

"Crazy is a good word for it," Tully agreed.

"Personally, I would accept 'fucked up' as well," Penn said. "This is not what they fucking mean when they say a band killed it in a particular venue."

I would have laughed, but it wasn't funny right now. It might not be funny later, but I'd see how things went before I decided.

Meanwhile, if whoever was after us today was that desperate, they wouldn't hold back, or stop to ask questions. Unless they were here to check our visa status. We could be overreacting.

Yeah, okay, I didn't buy that either.

Standing up and shouting, 'I'm not a Brantley,' wouldn't save my ass. Or anyone else's. None of us would do that anyway. We wouldn't throw Zeke under the bus.

"So, the little wolves have fled," a male voice said from the stage. "Let me introduce myself, since this is my shit show now. My name is Sutton Fiorelli. You might know my name. You were acquainted with my sister, Renae."

He must have had some theatre training, because he was good at throwing his voice. Of course, the acoustics in the stadium were designed for that.

Yeah, Abbie, I told myself. *How about you* don't *be impressed by the bad guy?*

"We didn't have a problem with you, only with the twins," Sutton went on. "But you had to go and wage war on us, didn't you?"

"Fucking idiot," Penn muttered. "He sounds like a cartoon villain."

I swallowed down a laugh and then bit back a cough. Nothing would give me away faster than, I don't know, making a shit load of noise.

"In case you're wondering, I brought more people with me than my sister did. We have the backstage area secured. We know you're up there.

You have nowhere to go. You might as well come down. In case you think I'm joking, or that the gun I brought isn't loaded, let's have a little demonstration."

He raised the gun and turned in a slow circle, looking at each of the instruments already set up on the stage.

Penn groaned softly. "Fucking don't."

Sutton aimed the gun at Penn's precious keyboard and pulled the trigger. And again. And again. The bullets found their marks with heart-breaking accuracy, shattering the keys and sending plastic and metal flying.

"I'm going to—"

I grabbed Penn's arm before he could jump up and run back down to the stage.

It was Tully who hissed, "You have others."

Even if he didn't, his instrument wasn't worth dying for. Not the musical one anyway. I got it though. This was nothing but vandalism. Destruction of a perfectly good keyboard just because he could. I bet he had the smallest cock known to humankind.

"Don't care about that?" Sutton taunted. He nodded to one of his cronies.

Tully made a soft growl in the back of his throat

as the man put his gun away and picked up one of Tully's guitars.

He said something that sounded like, "I've always wanted to do this," and smashed the guitar into the stage.

I glanced over at Tully. His fingertips were pressed to his forehead. He shook his head. He looked like he wanted to do some smashing of his own, but heads, not instruments. Obviously.

Tully lowered his hand. "Come with me." He gestured towards me and Penn.

For once, no one made a joke. If Penn noticed the innuendo, he gave no sign. He just waved at me to move between him and Tully.

I swallowed and followed the guitarist further up through the shadows amongst the seats. I don't know how he knew, but he led us straight to Asher and Zeke. Ninja skills, presumably.

Where were Landon, Channing and Jackson? I peered through the darkness, but saw no sign of them. Presumably, they were well hidden. Hopefully together.

I crept over to Asher and let him give me a quick hug.

"Thank fuck," he whispered. "I was worried about you."

"I was worried about me too," I said. Now probably wasn't the time for joking, but my remark was met with a soft chuckle.

"You're a badass, nothing bad would have happened to you," Asher said with more confidence than I felt.

"Did you miss the armed assholes on the stage?" Penn hissed. Yeah, he wasn't going to forgive the damage to his keyboard anytime soon.

"No one missed them, Penny," Asher whispered.

"Stay here," Tully said softly.

"Where are you—" Penn started to say, but Tully melted into the shadows.

"Okay," Penn whispered slowly.

The asshole finished smashing Tully's guitar. The stadium filled with silence.

"Tully is not going to let that slip by," Asher said in my ear. His warm breath became a groan when Sutton turned his attention to Asher's drums.

"You can come out, or I can keep smashing," Sutton said.

What sort of offer was that anyway? Sure the guys' instruments were precious to them, but not as precious as their own lives. Of course, it had nothing to do with the instruments or the guy's lives. It was retribution for what happened to Renae. Of course, the stupid butt plug wouldn't know it was Hunter who killed her and not one of us.

I wasn't going to be the one to tell him.

"Let's have some fun, shall we?" Sutton said slowly.

What he was doing up until now, I had no idea. He seemed as though he was having fun to me. Sick, twisted, fucking fun.

He scooped up Channing's saxophone from where it leaned against a box and drove the end of it into Asher's kick drum.

Asher looked away and pressed his face into my shoulder.

I patted his back as reassuringly as I could.

"That felt so good," Sutton said. "Not as good as hitting one of you guys with it, but close enough." For good measure, he slammed the saxophone into the stage and then stepped on the mouthpiece. Would he have done that if he knew who he was fucking with? Probably. A guy like him wouldn't be intimidated by Channing, even if he knew what he'd done.

"This is just foreplay, of course," Sutton said.

"How to say you don't know how to please your partner without saying you don't know how to please your partner," Asher said in my ear.

Once again, I had to choke back a laugh. It was one thing to use humour to get you through the dark times, and another thing to die for it. I strenuously objected to losing my life for a chuckle. I poked Asher in the ribs to tell him to stop it.

He jerked, but fell silent.

"This is my way," Sutton continued, "of killing time while waiting. Waiting for what, I'm sure you're wondering." He paced from one side of the stage to the other slowly, like he was out for a pleasant stroll in the garden. If he did that, the plants would probably wilt around him.

Whatever it was we were waiting for, I was sure we wouldn't like it. I doubted it would be anything good. It never was with people like him. Couldn't he just come to us with a box of chocolates and a pleasant conversation? Fuck no, they had to go all shooting and smashing shit.

Footsteps sounded from backstage, heading up slowly.

"That isn't ominous at all," Asher whispered.

I poked him again.

He twitched and grabbed my finger to stop me from doing it again. I had another hand if I needed to use it.

"Shhh," Zeke hissed. He peered between two seats.

Five more people stepped up on stage. Three I recognised, two I didn't.

Jackson, Landon and Channing, followed by an older man and a younger one, both with guns in their hands. The guys looked unharmed, for now, but pissed off. Channing especially, when he saw what they'd done to his saxophone. He looked as though when he was done with them, they'd be lucky to be recognisable.

Landon was sticking close to Channing's side, and Jackson, being Jackson, put himself between them and the bad guys.

"Have you warmed the crowd up?" the older man asked.

"Hey, Dad," I think they're ready for you."

I squinted at the stage. Things must be getting desperate if they needed—

"Dante Fiorelli," Zeke whispered.

CHANNING

"This way," I said.

When Zeke told us all to scatter, I grabbed Landon and did just that. I went to grab Abbie as well, but Jackson had her by the hand and they seemed to be following Zeke.

Instead of heading into the stands, we headed out a side door, Landon's hand sweaty in mine.

"What the hell?" Landon panted.

"I don't know; I'm not sticking around to find out." I wasn't a fan of guns, especially when they were aimed at me or anyone I loved.

I pulled Landon behind a pile of boxes that would have contained some of our rigging, and tried to get a handle on what was going on. Where should we go? How many bad guys were there? After the altercation in LA, I assumed there were more of them than we faced there. They might have thought we were a pushover then, but they knew better now. None of us was going down without a fight.

I saw someone walk past and ducked down lower.

"Go out on stage and take those two with you," a voice ordered. An older man, someone with authority over the others. Asshole didn't intimidate me, but judging by the way he spoke, he was used to intimidating the people around him. He reminded me of Reuben and my father. People determined to get their own way no matter who they had to fuck over to get there.

I glanced over at Landon's pale face. He looked like he was going to pee his pants, but he really wasn't. He was stronger than he knew and now was the time for him to prove it. To himself. I already knew he was a badass.

I put my fingers to my lips and pointed forward. If we stayed behind the boxes, no one would see us. Once we got to the other end, we could figure out where to go from there. With any luck, we'd have a free run to the door leading out to the rig truck.

Landon nodded and turned to walk away in a crouch.

It was slow going, but I stayed on his tail, my ears and eyes open. On the other side of the boxes, people walked past, stopping to talk in low voices, before they moved on. I tried to get some idea of how many there were, but without being able to see them, it would only be a guess. I could safely assume they were all armed and ready to use them.

I kept an eye out for a weapon, but the fucking tour staff were meticulous in tidying up as they went. Levi and Jackson insisted on it. Right now, we could have used a pipe or something. Hell, I'd give anything for a spray can and a cigarette lighter. A homemade flamethrower would be useful. Better yet, a bazooka or even a handgun.

At times like this, we usually joked about a cloak of invisibility, but there wasn't anything funny about the situation. There would be plenty of time for joking later.

We reached the end of the boxes and I gestured for Landon to stay down. He looked like he wanted to argue, but his brow was covered in a sheen of sweat. Even when his mother was being a bitch I'd never seen him truly scared, until now.

Just hold it all together until we get through this, I thought. *You can freak the fuck out afterwards.* And then we could get nice and drunk.

I patted his shoulder for reassurance, then slowly rose.

"Hello there." I found the barrel of a gun pointed right at my face.

Fuck.

"Hey," I said. Landon would have said something clever like he'd dropped some money behind here or we crept away to fuck. Me, I couldn't think of anything smart to say. So instead I said, "What the fuck do you want?"

"Let's start with you coming out of there." He was the older man, late forties, maybe early fifties, a generous sprinkling of grey in his hair. Lines around his eyes matched the ones around his mouth. His skin looked like it tanned too often, and time was catching up with him. He was relatively attractive for someone holding a firearm in my face.

Fucker.

"Keep your hands up where I can see them," he said as I stepped out from behind the boxes. "You too." He gestured in Landon's direction. "I know there's at least two of you behind there."

"Congratulations," I said sarcastically.

He gave me a look that suggested I should probably not be a smartass to someone with a weapon, but I couldn't help myself. If I made him angry enough, maybe I could find a way to disarm him.

Landon crab walked to the side of the boxes and slowly rose.

"See, that wasn't so hard, was it?" the man said.

"I've met people like you," I said. "Doing shit like this makes them hard."

He chuckled. "That's true, but at my age you want things sorted quickly so you can go and have a nice glass of whiskey."

"We're not stopping you," I said. "If you want to leave, there's the door." I jerked my head toward it.

"Not until I've finished what I came here for," he said.

"So you know, the Brantley twins aren't here," I said. Let's be real here, they could have snuck up at any point, the pair of slippery pricks. But as far as I knew, I was telling the truth.

He shrugged one shoulder. "I cared about that before you killed my daughter."

I blinked a couple of times. "Your— Oh. So you know, that wasn't us. I mean, we were there, but it was Hunter Brantley who killed her."

"That may be true," he agreed, "and it may not. But you were there and that makes you accountable."

That was some fuzzy, fucking logic right there.

"No offence, but I think you're reaching a bit. That's like saying the audience is responsible for a football team losing." I was going to say, 'or us sucking,' but we rarely sucked these days. Not in a bad way anyway.

"I'd also like to point out, she was trying to kill us," I said.

"When she died she wasn't," Landon said helpfully. "She made peace with us, then Hunter killed her." Apparently that was the wrong thing to say, because Dante poked him in the side with his gun.

Landon flinched. His eyes were wide with fear, but he managed not to make a sound. I was proud of him, he was keeping it together.

Just a bit longer, I thought.

I desperately wanted to drive my fist into the old man's face, but I grabbed Landon's arm and pulled him to me instead.

"He's right, but we'll do as you say until we can get all of this sorted out," I said quickly.

His face red with anger, Dante said, "You can start by shutting up."

I nodded and squeezed Landon's arm. He nodded too, more vigourously than I had.

"Good, now go that way." Dante waved the gun in the direction we had come from. I sighed, but did as he asked. Right now, the best way to stay alive was to go along with their bullshit.

We only made it a few steps before one of his minions called out, "Boss, I found another one."

We all turned and I had to suppress a groan. A man about my age had Jackson at gunpoint. He looked unimpressed but uninjured. So far.

I shot him a questioning look. Where the fuck was Abbie?

He shook his head, he didn't know. Not dead then. They must have gotten separated in the scramble. No doubt she was with the other guys. They better be keeping her safe or they'd have me to answer to.

"Back inside the stadium, gentlemen," Dante said. He nodded and his minion waved for Jackson to walk beside us.

We were herded through another door into the backstage area, to the stairs which lead up to the stage. It wasn't until then I realised I'd heard some loud, disconcerting sounds coming from there.

When I stepped out onto the stage I realised why.

My fucking beautiful saxophone. It wasn't beyond repair, but I wouldn't be playing it tonight. Neither would Asher with his kick drum, Tully with his guitar and... Were those bullet holes in

Penn's keys? He was going to be pissed as fuck about that.

"Hey, Dad, I think they're ready for you." The speaker was a couple of years older than me, with a passing resemblance to Dante.

Oh good, another Fiorelli brat. Another one I should have killed when I had the chance.

"I thought you would have rounded the rest of them up by now," Dante said, his tone full of condemnation. Apparently junior was a disappointment. What a shame.

Sutton's smile slipped. "I was working on it, but then I thought you might want the honours."

I glanced at Landon and rolled my eyes. And we thought our guys were full of shit. This Sutton prick failed and he knew it. The fun part was, his father knew it too. Good, let them gnaw at each other. It might give us an in.

"We have the place locked down," one of the minions said. "We know the rest of them are in here." He made it sound like it was a small deal, not a stadium with a capacity of fifty-four thousand people.

"They'll come out when we start killing," Dante said. He eyed each of us speculatively. His gaze lingered on Jackson, who stood a bit in front us.

Evidently his attempt to protect us, subtle and unnecessary as it was, hadn't gone unnoticed.

I started as a grinding noise echoed through the stadium. I took my eyes off Dante's gun long enough to look upwards.

The stadium's retractable roof was starting to close. Slow at first but gradually moving more quickly, blocking out the last of the evening light. We were almost in darkness except for the lights all around the edges of the stadium, and those in the rigging.

"They must have listened to my warning about rain coming," Jackson said. "It took them long enough." He looked so irritated I almost believed him. If I didn't know him so well, I wouldn't have guessed he was stalling. What was he stalling for though?

His expression gave away absolutely nothing. I made a note never to play poker with him. Not that I played poker anyway, but his poker face was on point.

Dante looked like he wasn't sure if he should believe him, but apparently the roof closing wasn't on his list of concerns right now. He shrugged and moved around behind Jackson, his gun hanging loosely in his hand.

"Your boy tells me Hunter Brantley killed my daughter," he said.

Landon twitched at being referred to as a boy, but thank fuck, he kept his mouth closed.

Jackson's tongue darted over his lips and he nodded. "Yes, that's accurate."

"Who killed those working with her?" Dante moved around slowly.

Jackson swallowed. "It was a combination of—"

Dante stopped to kick Landon's guitar so hard we all startled. It fell and lay on the stage, undamaged as far as I could tell. Lucky for him or he would die more slowly for upsetting Landon. "Who killed them?"

"We did," Jackson said. "In self defence."

"So you admit culpability?" Dante demanded.

"I admit to people dying so we could save our asses," Jackson said evenly. "Your personal narrative might look at it differently."

"My personal narrative," Dante echoed, "has decided you can be the first to pay for what happened to my daughter." He raised the gun to Jackson's temple.

With a mechanical clunk all the lights in the stadium went out.

23

ABBIE

WE WERE PLUNGED INTO DARKNESS. Not absolute, but fucking close enough.

A second or two later, a shot rang out across the stadium. I recognised the slight muffled sound made by a silencer, but it still sounded like a crack of thunder.

I had barely enough time to take a breath before I heard a thud and panicked scrambling from down on the stage.

"That's our cue," Zeke said. "Penn, stay here with Abbie. Asher, let's go."

"What—" Penn started to say.

"Tully," I said softly.

Zeke's teeth flashed in the dark. "Who else?"

I should have realised when the roof closed that

the guitarist was behind it. He must have gotten into the control booth. With a whole shit ton of luck, I'd get to ask him about that later.

Strong hands pressed against my cheeks and Asher kissed me. "Love you. Stay safe."

"Love you too," I said. "You better not die or I'll…" Be heartbroken. We'd been through too much to lose each other now.

"We won't," Zeke said. "I love you."

"I love you," I said before he crept away.

Someone let out a cry of pain, but it didn't sound like any of my guys. Or maybe that was wishful thinking.

I peeked between two seats but couldn't make out anything other than dark shapes moving around. Either no one down there thought to put their phone torch on, or they didn't want to make themselves a target.

I put a hand over my mouth and leaned against Penn as realisation crept into my brain. Dante Fiorelli was holding a gun to Jackson's head right before the light went out. That thud…

I swallowed down a sob but a tear trickled down my cheek, followed by another one. Never in my life have I ever wanted to kill anyone. Until now. If I had a gun in my hand and Dante Fiorelli in front of me, I wouldn't be able to stop myself from using it.

I thought back to our band outing to the shooting range, and how the guys taught me to use a gun and told me the dangers of panicking and being emotional with a weapon in your hand. They never told me I might get emotional because someone I loved was killed, and burning rage would take over my heart.

Penn exhaled next to my ear.

"Are we really going to stay up here out of the way?" he asked.

I looked up at him and jumped as another shot rang out. That was followed by a short cry and a gurgling sound, then another thud.

"Zeke will—" I started.

"Be grateful for any help he can get if we save his ass," Penn finished for me. "You know what, you're right. You should stay here. You'll be safe out of the way. Just like I've been saying since before the tour."

He was clearly trying to get a rise out of me. It worked.

"You're still an asshole," I told him.

"Hell yeah, I am," he said. He pressed his forehead to mine. "I love you. You're a pain in the ass, but you're my pain in the ass."

"I love you too, even though you're a jerk." I lightly kissed his mouth. "Okay, let's go and kick some butt."

He took my hand and we rose. There was so much noise and scuffling coming from the stage, we didn't bother trying to be quiet. We took the stairs as quickly and carefully as we could. Nothing would reveal our presence quicker than us tumbling down the stairs. Not to mention that we might hurt ourselves. That would suck.

We were about three rows from the front when the same metallic clunk echoed through the stadium and the lights came back on.

Penn yanked me behind the row of seats. "Looks like time's up."

I grunted in pain as I fell on my knees and squinted against the sudden glare.

Either Tully turned the lights back on or the stadium staff had. Either way, we were now bathed in light.

"What's going on?" I was too scared to look for myself. With wide eyes, I looked over at Penn.

He had a grim expression on his face, but looked over the armrest in front of him. Without answering my question, he said, "Wait here." He scrambled out of the row and down towards the stage.

"What the fuck?" I said to empty space. I might have done what he said and stayed put, but by now it's well documented that I don't do what I'm told.

I snuck back to the end of the row and looked around.

The stage was packed, and an absolute mess. Sutton Fiorelli lay near Asher's drums, a gaping hole in his chest. That must have been his death gurgle.

Sorry, not sorry.

Dante Fiorelli and one of his minions had guns in their hands. So did Landon and—oh my god—Jackson. He looked a little rough and messy—and kinda hot—but he was alive.

"Looks like we have a stand-off," Zeke said. He stood at the edge of the stage, his hand around the neck of Tully's guitar. Judging by the still forms of two minions who lay near him, he'd used it on them.

Desperate times, I guess.

"They're outnumbered," Asher pointed out.

"We'll take a few of you with us," Dante said.

"How about you don't?" Penn said. He raised a hand as though shrugging, but I got the impression he was waving at something in particular.

I looked over in that direction and noticed a side door. I bit my lip. Was he suggesting what I thought he was suggesting?

No, he was just telling me to get the fuck out of the stadium.

I had other ideas.

I crawled down to the end of the row, and peeked out again.

From this angle, Dante and his minion had their backs to me. Silently, and keeping as low as I could, I snuck out from behind the chairs and darted out the door.

I found myself in an empty hallway that led out of the stadium. The other direction led backstage. During a concert, the doors would be closed and locked to prevent groupies from sneaking in. Since the tour staff were still setting up, the doors were open, a box placed in front of one to stop it from swinging shut.

Aware there might be other minions around, I trotted to the door and glanced inside.

"What are you doing here?" Tully whispered behind me.

I jumped about a thousand feet in the air and whirled around, my hand to my chest. "You scared the shit out of me."

He smiled briefly. "I could have been anyone."

"No one else would have snuck up like that without me seeing you," I pointed out.

"That's an assumption that could have gotten you killed," he said. He grabbed my arm and pulled me back and off to the side. "What's going on up there?"

I told him in a handful of words and he nodded.

"Looks like time to break up a stand-off."

"Is this where you tell me to stay here," I asked. "Because I—"

"No, I need you along on this," he said. "But I'm going to need you to do what I say. It's the only way we'll get out of here alive." He gave me a long, firm look, his brown eyes boring into mine.

I nodded. "Okay." No pressure. If I fucked up and got someone killed I would never forgive myself. A few short weeks ago, the only thing on the line was my career. Now it was my whole heart and all seven guys that each owned a bit of it.

"Good. Stay behind me and keep your eyes and ears open. I've taken care of most of his people, but there might be one or two left wandering around."

That explained the sheen of sweat on his brow. If he had any blood on him, he was hidden by the colour of his shirt. He looked good in black, and right now I was glad he wore it. If he was covered in blood, I would freak out right now.

"Do you trust me?" he asked.

"Of course I do," I said without hesitation. Maybe

I shouldn't be so hasty, but I really did. I trusted whatever he had in mind, it was in all our best interests.

"Good. Come on then." He started to walk toward the backstage area, every movement cautious and deliberate. This wasn't the laid-back, gentle Tully I knew. This was Tully in stealth mode. It was sexy as fuck.

I tried to copy the way he moved, but probably looked ridiculous. Whatever, right now I was a hot pink ninja, ready to save my guys if I could.

We reached the steps and Tully dropped to a crouch. He gestured for me to do the same.

I crouched beside him and we listened.

"You know it's over, Fiorelli," Channing was saying. "You're totally fucked. Put down the gun and we might let you walk out of here alive. Your problem isn't with us, it's with the Brantley twins. We could just forget all of this and move on."

And send you the bill for all the destruction, I thought.

"You said Landon and Jackson had guns, didn't you?" Tully whispered in my ear.

I nodded and gave him a questioning look. What did that have to do with anything? Apart from the fact...

My mouth formed an O. They were the two least likely to kill anyone. Would Fiorelli know that? Probably. Predators like him were good at reading people.

Tully must have seen my realisation, because he bobbed his head quickly and turned his attention back to the stage. I could almost see the wheels turning in his brain.

"Enough of this," Dante snapped. "We both know you're not going to use those on us. You're just wasting time until the rest of my people come and dispose of you." He sounded very certain that was going to happen.

"Stand up," a voice said behind us.

I startled, but before I could move a hair, Tully had leapt up and swept the legs out from under the minion who crept up on us.

He grunted as he landed heavily on his back. The gun slid out of his hand.

I scrambled to my feet and ran to scoop it up. "You have some reflexes," I said to Tully.

He flashed me a grin and drove the heel of his boot into the man's throat. There wasn't even time for a gurgle, just a crunch of bone and a squelch I'd hear until the day I died.

I looked away as blood sprayed onto the carpet.

Holy shit.

The sound must have been audible from the stage, because I caught movement in the corner of my eye.

I looked up and saw Dante Fiorelli looking down at me. His eyes were the bluest I'd ever seen, contrasting with his black hair. He reminded me of Pete.

I didn't think.

I didn't hesitate.

I raised the gun, aimed it and fired.

An expression of shock crossed his features at the same time as blood blossomed across his groin. He opened his mouth as though he was going to shout something but then slowly, like time slowed, he fell. He landed on the surface of the stage with a thump and a groan.

I was vaguely aware of another shot and Fiorelli's minion joined his boss on the floor.

The gun dropped out of my hand and my knees gave way under me. Tully caught me before I hit the ground, my mind churning, the world a haze around me.

Blood pounded through my body.

The only thing I could think was— *I killed a man.*

24

ABBIE

"I'M GUESSING that wasn't what you had in mind?" I asked.

"Not exactly." Tully raised his glass to me. "But it got the job done."

I raised my glass back and swallowed a gulp of wine.

We all looked over as Jackson entered the hotel room. He rubbed a hand over his face and blinked a couple of times. He looked rumpled and tired. Basically how I felt.

"The press and fans have accepted the bomb scare excuse," he said. "Fans are disappointed, but they understand why police are swarming all over the stadium. We should be clear for you to play tomorrow night, if you're up to it. "

"We'll be up to it," Zeke said. "If Asher is over his hangover by then."

"Hey," Asher said in protest. "I haven't had that much to drink."

"Yet," Penn said. He reclined against a wall, half of his attention on us and the other half on the news that was playing on the TV. I caught a glimpse of the stadium on the screen, and the faces of disappointed fans.

"They're the real victims here," Asher said. "I still can't believe you shot Dante Fiorelli in the cock."

"I was pretending it was Penn," I joked weakly. I glanced over at him and smiled, remembering his comment at the shooting range. He accused me of thinking about his cock while hitting the target in the groin. He was right, but I'd never tell.

"Remind me to teach you to aim for shoulders instead," Zeke said. "Shooting a guy in the cock is a dangerous reflex for a girl to have."

"It looked like a painful way to die." Landon still looked slightly freaked out from the evening's attack. He was snuggled up to Channing, but something in the way they sat looked comfortable, not like Landon was scared he was going to leave, and needed to hold him down.

"It couldn't have happened to a better mother-fucker," Penn said.

"What Penn said," Channing said.

Penn raised an eyebrow at him. "Did you just agree with me?"

"Just this once," Channing said. "I still want that race do-over. The sooner I can kick your ass, the better."

I slipped out of my seat and walked over to put my arms around Jackson. "They're never going to change, are they?"

"You wouldn't want us to change," Tully said. "Either of you."

"I guess not," I agreed. I turned back to Jackson. "Are you okay?"

"For someone who was almost shot in the head, I'm doing fine," he said. "How about you? You must be... Conflicted?"

I thought about that for a moment. "Kinda. I mean, he wasn't walking out of there alive and he would have happily taken as many of you with him as he could."

"It was awesome," Asher said. "I wish I'd done it, but it was still fucking epic. Hey, Jackson, how did you not get shot?"

"He threw himself into us," Channing said. "Dude has one move, but it's a good one."

I glanced back at Jackson as he shrugged.

"I think it's a good idea to get out of the way of a bullet and get you guys out of the firing line at the same time. Wouldn't every manager do that?" He gave me a lopsided smile which made my heart flip.

"That's a resounding no," I said dryly. "Hopefully it's nothing you'll ever have to do again."

"The Fiorellis will be in disarray now," Zeke said. "Reuben can take care of the rest of it. They should leave us alone now to enjoy the rest of the tour."

"I'll drink to that," Asher said, raising his beer bottle high.

The rest of the guys matched him.

I sighed. "What happens after the tour?" I asked Jackson. I searched his denim blue eyes, hoping he had some answers.

"After the tour is IslandFest," he said. "Levi expects you to join the boys there. I was thinking maybe you and I could… I don't know, I'll arrange something."

I felt my face heat. "I'd like that."

"Good, because I hear you were talking to Levi and suggested we get our band back together for one last concert there too." He raised an eyebrow at me.

"I—" I blushed a little brighter. "I just thought… You two might enjoy playing again. If only one more time in front of an audience."

He smiled. "I can't wait. I wish I thought of it myself. It's exactly what I need after all this craziness. I'm not surprised you know what I need more than I do." He sounded a little choked up.

I kissed his mouth.

He kissed me back but then reluctantly broke off. "I have to go and speak to Levi. He needs to know what went on here. I was thinking I might suggest that nothing changes."

I gave him a funny look. A confused glance over shoulder showed all the guys were looking at him the same way too.

"What do you mean?" I asked softly.

"I mean, you touring with the guys is unorthodox but it's working. I don't see a reason not to do it again. Without all the killing and stalking and shit."

I grinned. "I like the sound of that." We could have our break time together and travel the world together. What could be better than that?

"Or she could officially join Wolf Venom?" Penn suggested.

Everyone looked at him in surprise. He'd come a

long way from the guy who claimed he didn't want me around at all.

"Or that," Zeke agreed.

I thought about that for a moment. "I'd love to, but I still have my career to rebuild. I've just started getting that on track. There's still a ways to go." Plus I wanted to keep my creative freedom. I'd have more of that as a soloist than I would as a part of the band. And I'd get to jam with them. Win-win.

Zeke and Penn both nodded. Neither looked surprised, or annoyed. I didn't think they would be. They supported me and my career one hundred percent. That was just another reason I loved them. One of so many.

"We will need to work out where we're all going to live," Zeke said.

"I vote one big house with a cuddle puddle," Asher said.

"And a sensory room," Tully added.

"And recording studio," Landon said.

"And a gun range," Channing said.

"And a soundproof room where I can go to get away from you motherfuckers," Penn said.

"And a pool," Zeke said. "I've always wanted to live somewhere with a pool."

"I'll leave you to work that out." Jackson gave me a quick kiss and slipped back out the door.

"In the meantime," Penn turned off the TV and stepped over to me, "I don't know about you guys, but I'd like to celebrate being alive." He slipped his arms around me from behind.

EPILOGUE

ABBIE

I GLANCED around Reuben's library while the guys talked. He had more books than he had the last time I was here. I'd like to think someone with so many books couldn't be irredeemably evil, but it was Reuben we were talking about. He'd always be an asshole.

"And so you hid when you saw Fiorelli coming?" Asher asked Hunter. He looked like he was trying not to laugh at him.

Hunter gave him a look. "We were on our way, okay?" His eyes flicked over to Reuben, who sat in his big leather chair, looking unimpressed.

"Would you believe we got lost on the way?" Parker asked.

"Nope," Zeke said easily. "I'm with Asher. You took one look at them and ran away."

"We did not—" Hunter started to protest.

"That sounds accurate," Reuben said, his tone as dark as his expression.

"At least I got rid of Renae Fiorelli," Hunter said sulkily.

"Yes, at least you got rid of an unarmed woman who basically surrendered," Zeke said.

"She would have come after you again anyway," Parker said. "Having her there might have tipped the scales against you."

I could tell from their expressions no one believed a word the twins were saying. Whatever. That was firmly in the, 'not my problem,' basket. They made their beds, now they got to lie in them.

Reuben turned to Zeke. "I commend you for dispatching Dante Fiorelli and his son, Sutton."

"It was Abbie who killed Dante," Zeke said evenly. "We don't know exactly who killed Sutton. With the lights out, it could have been anyone. Including Dante."

We'd discussed this a couple of times since that night, so I wasn't surprised by the suggestion. Dante certainly hadn't seemed impressed by his son. But to kill him? That was another thing that wasn't my problem. These people were all kinds of fucked up. If they wanted to take each other out, then so be it.

I was distracted by the sound of footsteps in the corridor outside the library. They stopped just outside the door.

Without moving, Reuben said, "You can come in."

I wouldn't have believed he was capable of talking in such a soft tone if I hadn't heard him myself. I found myself blinking at him in surprise before I glanced toward the door.

A woman around my age, stepped into the doorway. She looked tentative, nervous. Dark hair hung to her waist. Her large blue eyes had a hint of green. She was at least six or seven months pregnant.

Asher shot out of his chair. "Mina?"

It took a minute for that to register. Mina? As in his *sister* Mina? What had he said about her? *'We used to call her Mina Sunshine, because she was always smiling.'*

She wasn't smiling now. She looked anxious, like a scared rabbit looking at a fox. Or a den of foxes.

"Hello, Asher," she said softly.

Asher's gaze dropped to her belly. "Whose baby is that?"

Silence fell except the slow, heavy tick of a clock on the wall.

It was broken by a single word from Reuben. "Mine."

THANKS FOR READING. Wold Venom has one last adventure in the novella Venomous! For more dark romance set in the Wolf Venom world, check out Bait.

Reuben's story is coming in 2024!

I hope you loved Saving Abbie as much as I loved writing the books. If you did, leave a review, tell your friends, make a viral video!

Maggie Alabaster writes reverse harem and, paranormal, sci-fi and fantasy romance.

She lives in NSW, Australia with one spouse, two daughters, one dog, and countless birds.

Jo Bradley writes contemporary romance.

Sign up for Maggie's newsletter! Sign Up!

Join Maggie's reader group! Join here!

Follow Maggie on Bookbub! Click here to follow me!

Check out Maggie's website- www. maggiealabaster.com

Sign up for Jo's newsletter

Join Jo's reader group Jo Bradley's Book Addicts

Follow Jo on Bookbub

Dark Masque

Book 1 Bait

Book 2 Prey

Book 3 Trap

Saving Abbie

Book 1 Pitch

Book 2 Pound

Book 3 Session

Book 4 Muse

Book 5 Rhythm

Book 6 Encore

Novella Venomous

Ruthless Claws

Book 1 Ivory

Book 2 Crimson

Book 3 Elodie

Harmony's Magic

Book 1 Summoned by Fire

Book 2 Summoned by Fate

Book 3 Summoned by Desire

Shifter's Vault

Book 1 Discarded

Book 2 Deceived

Book 3 Disgraced

My Alien Mates

Book 1 Star Warriors

Book 2 Star Defenders

Book 3 Star Protectors

Academy of Modern Magic

Book 1 Digital Magic

Book 2 Virtual Magic

Book 3 Logical Magic

Complete Collection

Summer's Harem

Book 1: Shimmer

Book 2: Glimmer

Book 3: Flicker

Complete collection

Short reads

Taken by the Snowmen

Jingle All the Way

Also by Maggie Alabaster and Erin Yoshikawa

Caught by the Tide

Book 1–Pursued by Shadows

Book 2 Pursued by Darkness

Book 3 Pursued by Monsters